The Gnome Door Chronicles

By Tom Dillman

Copyright © 2020 by Tom Dillman
Cover Copyright © 2020 Crave Press

All rights reserved, including the right to reproduce the book or portions thereof in any form or by any means, electronic or mechanical, including photocopying, recording, or by any information storage and retrieval system, without permission in writing from the publisher. All inquiries should be addressed to Crave Press, Leesport PA.

Printed in the United States of America

SECOND EDITION

ISBN: 978-0-9977949-7-7

Published by:

Crave Press

www.cravepress.com

Chapter 1

Susan emptied her backpack on the bed and checked everything inside.

Her pack carried enough clothes for three days, a few camping supplies, and her lunch. Her ultra-light sleeping bag and a mini tent were strapped to the outside of the pack.

Mina's voice contained a trace of impatience as she said, "Susan, you've repacked that backpack at least fifteen times. It's only a weekend camping trip, and you've gone on these trips with your grandfather before. You're used to hiking with that pack, and your grandfather has most of the supplies. I promise you that you have everything that you need. *And* you're leaving in twenty minutes. Would you please relax?"

Mina was right. Mina was almost always right. Mina was Susan's grandfather's housekeeper, and from the very first day that Mina had come to live here, she always seemed to know what was best for them.

The last two years would have been a lot harder for Susan if not for Mina. First, there was the split between her parents. Susan was still unhappy about the divorce, but she understood the reason that they just couldn't live together anymore. She also understood that her parents loved her. They both had great jobs, but they were both required to travel a lot. Her father was the vice president of a large import company and her mother was a consultant for a travel agency. That's how they met. Unfortunately, there were constant conflicts over their schedules, and Susan was always stuck in the middle. Eventually they were arguing all the time, and they both knew that they had to do what was best for Susan and get divorced.

So Susan and her mom went to live with her grandparents. Even before she came to live there, Susan had already spent most of her summers at her grandparents' home. She loved her grandparents and their big old house with the wide open spaces. The nearest neighbor was a mile down the road. Susan already had her own room, so coming to stay there was an easy transition. After a little redecorating, (that Bon Jovi poster just had to go), her mom moved back into her old room and lived there with them whenever she wasn't traveling. Susan's father always set aside the last two weeks of summer to spend with her, and her grandparents set up the small cottage on the edge of the property for him to stay in whenever he could. Actually, her parents seemed to get along much better after the separation, and they both agreed that having Susan live with her grandparents was the most stable environment for her.

Then Grandma Anna got sick. When Susan was younger, her mother had tried to get her to use the more formal titles of grandmother and grandfather. Her grandfather was fine with that, and the name Grandfather quickly changed from a polite title to a term of endearment. Her grandmother wouldn't hear of being addressed so formally. She said that she had grown up with fancy titles, and she wanted no parts of them anymore. She insisted on being called Grandma Anna, saying that she loved the sound of Susan's voice and as her grandmother, she had every right to choose any name she wished. Eventually, Susan's mother gave in and even started referring to her that way when she spoke of her.

Grandma Anna's doctors said she had an aggressive form of cancer. She got very weak very quickly, and she lost all her hair from the treatments. One day, she took Susan into town and let her help pick out the most outrageous hat that she could find. But she never lost her smile. No matter how much pain she was in, Grandma Anna always remained the kindest and sweetest person that Susan had ever known.

That's when Mina came to stay with them. Mina had been her grandmother's nurse throughout her illness and then stayed on as housekeeper after Grandma Anna was gone. Mina was tough and firm. She filled in a lot of the gaps left by Grandma Anna's passing. She kept the household going, even scolding Susan's mom and grandfather when they became too sad. Mina had coaxed and guided them into returning to a normal life while never letting them forget how wonderful Grandma Anna was, and they loved Mina for it.

And now, here she was telling Susan to relax. But Susan couldn't just relax. Grandfather was taking her to visit her newest friend, Bodkin. Bodkin had come and spent the afternoon with Susan a few times, but this was the first time that Susan was able to go and visit her. Visiting Bodkin wasn't quite like staying over at some of her other friend's houses. Bodkin wasn't like any other twelve year old girl that she'd ever met.

Bodkin was an elf girl who lived on the other side of the Gnome Door, that special passage that was hidden in her grandfather's workshop and led to a whole different world. Elves, fairies and, of course, gnomes lived in that world with dozens of other amazing creatures, some good and some not so good. Some were frightening and dangerous. A few of them were a little bit of both.

Not long ago, Susan had stumbled upon the fact that her grandfather was secretly the guardian who protected this side of the mystic door. Over the years, her grandfather had told her the most wonderful stories about the world on the other side of the Gnome Door. Susan had always believed that even though they were just made up stories, her grandfather was such a good storyteller that they almost sounded real. Now she was finding out that some of those stories were true. Grandfather had promised to tell her how he came to be the guardian, but he insisted on getting her mom's permission before he told her too much. She was a little angry when Grandfather told her that her mother knew about the Gnome Door and kept it from her, but she kind of understood when her mother admitted to her that she wanted to wait until Susan was a little older before she revealed the secrets about it. Susan's mother had promised to explain everything in person as soon as she got home. But her mother's job had her traveling non-stop lately, and waiting for her to come home was driving Susan crazy. To make it up to Susan, her mother had agreed to let her go and visit Bodkin this particular weekend. It was midsummer, and if they were lucky, they might get to see the fairies dance. The fairies only danced at the height of summer. If Susan had to wait, she would certainly miss it.

    In spite of his reluctance to talk about it, Susan had been able to coax some information about the land beyond the door from her grandfather. She knew that he had lived there for a time and studied magic while he was there. He had also admitted that there really had been a terrible war against the gremlins and he had fought alongside the elves, but he didn't like to speak of it. It brought back terrible memories. Although he refused to say why, he eventually returned home and assumed the duties of the guardian of the Gnome Door.

    When Susan thought about how much her life had changed since the first time that she met Bodkin, sometimes it made her head spin.

    It started out like a regular morning. She had gone into her grandfather's workshop looking for her boomerang. A few months earlier, Susan and her mom were having lunch near the park in town. There was a young man from Australia throwing boomerangs in the park. Susan thought that they were the coolest things that she had ever seen.

As soon as they finished lunch, Susan went over and asked the young man if she could try throwing one. He showed them how to throw one so that it would spin around in a circle and come back to her. Her mom even tried it a few times, and it turned into a fun afternoon together. Susan was certain that the young man was flirting with her mom. When they got home, Susan told her grandfather all about it. Grandfather could make almost anything out of wood, and a few days later, they looked up plans on her computer and he had made her a boomerang of her own that was just the right size for her. She practiced throwing it almost every day. Grandfather said that she was starting to get a pretty good pitching arm.

Her grandfather was off running a few errands on that day, and Susan knew that she wasn't supposed to be in the workshop when he wasn't there, but she knew exactly where she had left the boomerang and it would only take her a minute to get it.

Susan sniffed the air as she entered the shop. It was a habit that she had gotten into because her grandfather would always challenge her to tell him what type of wood he was working on just from the smell. Oak and pine were easy. He worked with them all the time. Cedar smelled like her grandmother's favorite quilt, and Susan loved the smell of cedar because of that. There was a faint smell of oak from the cabinet that her grandfather was working on the day before.

Susan loved being in the workshop. It was the most fascinating place that she had ever seen. There were antique tools on the wall and a big old workbench right in the middle of the room. Susan went straight to the small office that her grandfather had in the corner of the shop. It was another one of her favorite places. There was a big desk that her grandfather had made, and a cabinet with drawers full of interesting stuff. There was also the stone table. It was just a tall table with a space on top that held a collection of polished stones of all different sizes and colors. A few of the stones even had fossils in them. Grandfather could name them all. When you picked some of them up and turned them around, the light would make them look like they were changing colors. Well...all but one. There was one yellow stone that was very plain. It reminded her of honey, except it was dull in color. Grandfather said that it was special because it made all the other stones shine brighter.

But of all the interesting things in the workshop, there was one special place that Susan was always drawn to. On the wall, right next to the big door to her grandfather's office was a small door, only about eight inches tall. From the very first time she saw it, Susan had always been fascinated by Gnome Door.

The Gnome Door looked very old and had carvings around the frame that looked sort of like letters of the alphabet, but a little different. Grandfather called them runes, and said that they were magic symbols that prevented bad creatures from passing through the door into our world. Grandfather said that the Gnome Door was a portal, a special kind of doorway that allowed gnomes, elves, and other fairy creatures to travel back and forth from their world to ours. The world on the other side of the door was filled with magical creatures and beings.

The runes on the arch over the door were in a strange language, but her grandfather had told her what each one meant. The inscription over the door said, "Speak the word 'traveler,' and the portal shall open."

But it didn't say what the word was and, no matter how many times she asked, her grandfather would never tell her the right word. He would only smile at her and tell her that she would just have to figure it out for herself. Susan had tried every magic word that she could think of. Abracadabra, hocus pocus, and lots of other words. Nothing had ever worked.

When she was younger, Susan wanted to believe that the door was real, but she was starting to have some doubts. She had never seen any real magic. Maybe they were all just stories that her grandfather had made up to entertain her.

Susan automatically read the inscription as she approached the office and an idea suddenly occurred to her. What if the words on the door weren't just a greeting? What if they were instructions?

That was it! Suddenly Susan was sure that she knew the answer. It was so obvious. The magic word was right in front of her the whole time. She read the inscription again, just to be sure. "Speak the word 'traveler,' and the portal shall open."

Susan stood before the Gnome Door and in a clear voice said the word, "Traveler."

And nothing happened!

Susan couldn't believe it. She was positive that she had solved the riddle. How could she have been wrong?

Susan sighed as she turned and started to leave. Her grandfather's stories were all just stories. The door was just a carved piece of wood and there were no fairies or elves or magical creatures on the other side of the door.

She went back outside, feeling a little sad and disappointed.

As Susan walked across the yard, a faint blue light began to shine under the Gnome Door.

As Susan started across the back yard, she suddenly realized something. She had been so distracted with the Gnome Door that she had forgotten to get her boomerang. Now she had to go back inside again to get it. She wasn't supposed to be in there by herself in the first place, and now she had to go back a second time.

She would just dart in, grab the boomerang, and dash back out. She wouldn't even need to turn on the light. Susan slipped in through the door as quietly as possible and couldn't believe what she saw.

Tip-toeing across the floor was a tiny girl, no bigger than a doll. She was dressed all in green, and she carried a tiny bow.

The girl was looking the other direction and Susan whispered, "Boo."

The girl jumped and spun around. In the blink of an eye she pulled an arrow from the quiver that was slung over her shoulder. She knocked the arrow and pointed the bow straight at Susan.

Susan realized that she probably should have been frightened, but the girl was so small and delicate. And the way she was dressed, she looked sort of like someone from a video game.

Susan giggled. "I'm sorry. I didn't mean to really scare you."

The tiny girl stared at Susan intently. "Where is the guardian, child?"

Susan stood her ground and stared right back at the tiny girl. "Don't call me a child. My name is Susan, and I'm twelve years old. Almost a teenager. Besides, you don't look like you're much older than me."

The tiny bow never wavered as the girl spoke. "Don't let size fool you, child. I may be only twelve in your years, but I am a warden of the forest. Well...a warden in training."

Susan said to her, "Well, I'm sorry, 'Miss Warden in Training,' but I don't know anyone called the guardian."

"He is tall, with silver hair. He is a craftsman who works with wood in this place."

"Oh, he's not a guardian. That's just my grandfather and he's not here right now, and we shouldn't be in here either. Who are you and where did you come from? I was just here a minute ago and you weren't here then. And would you please stop pointing that bow and arrow at me?"

The tiny girl lowered the bow and said, "Well...you do seem rather harmless, and if the guardian is your grandfather, then I should be able to trust you. My name is Bodkin. I came through the portal."

"Oh, I don't believe that," said Susan. "You're trying to trick me. That's just a little fake door that my grandfather made. It's not real."

Bodkin looked at her in a strange way. "Are you so sure? I'll bet that your grandfather didn't tell you that."

"Well...no, he didn't. My mom did, but she said that Grandfather likes to pretend that the door is real, and I should play along."

"So who do you believe? Your mother or your grandfather? Perhaps you should just look for yourself, Susan, who is almost a teenager."

As the tiny girl called Bodkin said that, Susan suddenly noticed that there was something unusual around the corner by the office. As Susan approached the Gnome Door, she saw a blue light and realized that, not only had the door grown tall enough that she could have walked right through, but it was also open.

Magic! Real magic! The Gnome Door was real.

Susan looked through the open door and could see a small meadow surrounded by trees on the other side.

Bodkin's voice behind her asked, "Who do you believe now, Susan?"

Susan had been so surprised by the sight of the open door that she had momentarily forgotten about the tiny girl. "Oh, I'm so sorry that I didn't believe you. But, how did the door open? Why is it so big? And why are you here?"

Bodkin laughed at her. "You ask a lot of questions. The door opened because someone on this side said the right word. Every portal has a word that acts like a key and unlocks the door. When someone who can use magic says the proper word, the door will open and grow large enough for them to pass through. That's how portals work."

"But where does it go?" asked Susan.

"Into my world. People from your world call it Tir-Na-Fey. I believe that it means 'Land of Fairy' in one of this world's languages. You have so many here. Many of your legends come from something that lives in my world."

"That's exactly what my grandfather said," responded Susan.

"Fairies, gnomes, and many other creatures exist there," said Bodkin. "I'm from the Tek clan of Elves. My brother said that there used to be a lot of different clans, but they all united under one king long ago. Magic is common there. Sadly, there are also many evil creatures that would do terrible things if they were able to escape into your world."

Susan was a little frightened by the idea of monsters invading her world. "But what keeps them from coming here?"

"Don't they teach you anything in this world?" asked Bodkin. "My brother taught me all about your world years ago."

"Well, what makes him such an expert?" asked Susan. "And did your brother forget to teach you about manners?"

"Okay, I'm sorry. I didn't mean to be rude. One of his responsibilities is watching the other side of that door. He needs to know about your world."

"Okay, I'm sorry if I doubted him. Now, would you please tell me about the monsters?"

"Well, the worst of the evil creatures are trapped behind a magical wall known as the Barrier. It's hidden deep in the Dark Woods and surrounds the Land of Non. No one lives in the Dark Woods. It's a scary place. That's why it was chosen as the place to imprison these evil creatures. Long ago, a group of wizards aided by a number of dragons drove all the evil creatures into a secluded area of the Dark Woods and surrounded them with the magical wall that we call the Barrier. They named the place the Land of Non. Sometimes a creature does manage to get free. No one really knows how because the Barrier is supposed to be impenetrable, but if one of them should escape into your world, it could take years before they can be captured and brought back. The two worlds are normally separated by the fairy mists, and there are only a few special places with portals where someone can pass from one world to the other. When a door is opened by someone besides the guardian, the spirits who watch over the fairy mists can feel it. One of them will appear before a warden of the forest and warn them that a portal has been opened. The warden will come and meet with the guardian on this side to make sure that nothing evil passes through the portal. That's why I'm here."

"But didn't you say that you were only a warden in training?" asked Susan.

Bodkin blushed slightly. "Yes, my brother Pen is the regular warden. Our parents are gone, so the chief warden allows me to stay with him even though I'm too young to go into the regular training program. Early this morning, Pen had to go into the forest and check on the Golden Willow. Wysp went to find him when the door opened, but it may take him a few hours to get back."

Susan was becoming more confused by the minute. "What's a Golden Willow, and who's Wysp?"

"Your grandfather really hasn't told you anything," sighed Bodkin. "Wysp is a sprite. Pen says that sprites are a cross between an unruly child and an annoying insect, but sometimes they can be very helpful. If she wants to, she can make herself look like a little cloud with a face, but usually when she materializes, she's about as tall as your hand and looks like a young girl with wings. The edges of her wings are shaped like leaves so she can fold them around herself and hide in the trees when she doesn't want to be seen. She can move back and forth from one world to the other instantly."

"Wow, that must be fun. But what about the Golden Willow?" asked Susan.

"In the center of the forest, towering high over the rest of the trees is a magnificent tree with golden leaves. A dryad lives within the Golden Willow. A dryad is a spirit that's bonded to the tree. She's very old and knows many things that go on in the land. She passes what she can of her knowledge on to the elves to help keep the forest safe and healthy. She is also the source of great magic. One of the wardens of the forest goes there every week to speak with her and tend to her. This week, it was my brother's turn."

Susan's eyes lit up. "She sounds wonderful. I wish I could go and see this Golden Willow. Have you ever been there? Could you take me?"

"I have only been there once, when I was very young," answered Bodkin. "I would like to go again. It takes the good part of a day to hike there from here. If your grandfather allows it, maybe we could go together. But today, someone needs to stay and keep watch near the portal."

"But if your brother and my grandfather are both away, what can we do?"

"Well, Pen and I should have gotten word if any creatures had escaped from the behind the Barrier. So if you opened the door accidentally, there shouldn't be any real danger. The door will close by itself after a short time, but it needs to be sealed with magic. I will have to stay and watch this side of the door until either your grandfather or my brother returns."

"But what about the other side of the door?" asked Susan.

"I'm not really trained to do magic, but Pen showed me one trick that will hide the door and make it look like part of the hill. I'm not very good at it yet, and I don't know how long it will last. But that's the best that I can do. Wysp promised to help by keeping an eye on the other side of the door as soon as she returns from finding Pen. So as long as we stay close enough to see if anything approaches the door of your grandfather's workshop, and as long as Wysp doesn't get too distracted and wander off, we should be safe. Maybe while we wait, you can show me a little of your world."

While Susan watched, Bodkin darted back through the Gnome Door and exchanged her bow and arrows for a staff that she had hidden behind a nearby bush, then as she returned, she stopped and said three words in a language that Susan didn't recognize.

Now when Susan looked back through the portal, everything shimmered, almost like she was looking through the ripples on the surface of a pond. Just as they were starting toward the workshop door, Susan ducked back into the office and grabbed her boomerang.

"I'm not going to forget this again," she said.

Bodkin hesitated as they got near the door. "Is it safe for me to be out in the open? Someone from your world may see me."

"Yes, I think that we'll be okay," answered Susan. "Grandfather's yard is very big and the nearest neighbors are the retired couple that live two miles down the road. Mina, Grandfather's housekeeper, is the only other person within five miles. She has a bad leg and it hurts if she has to walk very far. She only comes all the way out to the workshop if she has to, and we could see her coming from far away."

"Okay, then why don't you show me that funny-looking stick that you seem so interested in?" said Bodkin, smiling.

Susan laughed and pointed to a spot a short distance from the workshop. "It's called a boomerang. If you stand over there, I'll show you what it does."

Susan moved out into the yard and faced away from Bodkin as she threw the boomerang. As soon as it left her hand, she knew that it was a good throw. It went out a short distance before it turned and lofted into a graceful arc. It looped around and gently landed a few feet from where Susan was standing. A perfect throw.

Bodkin's eyes lit up. "That was incredible. Is it a weapon?"

"Well, Grandfather did say that long ago, people used to hunt with them. A really good hunter could knock birds out of the air with them. But now, most people just throw them for sport."

"May I try it?" asked Bodkin eagerly.

"Of course you can try it. Come and stand over here."

Susan carefully showed her the proper way to stand and how to throw the boomerang so that it spun around.

It took Bodkin a few tries to figure out how to hold the boomerang with such small hands, and her first throws only went a short distance and then hit the ground. But Bodkin was a quick learner and a natural athlete. After a dozen throws, she got one with a good spin. And within twenty minutes, she could make it come back almost as well as Susan could.

They took turns throwing and seeing who could get the boomerang to land right at their feet without moving out of the way so it didn't hit them. Before they knew it, they had spent the whole morning together.

As Bodkin bent down to pick up the boomerang, she heard an unusual sound.

"What was that?"

Susan smiled. "That's just my phone. It's Mina. It must be lunchtime."

When Susan saw the confused look on Bodkin's face, she laughed. "You don't know what a phone is, do you? That must be one of the things that your brother didn't tell you about. It just lets me talk to someone who's far away. I'm only allowed to use it for emergencies and to talk to Mina. I'll show you, but you have to please be quiet or Mina will hear you." Susan pressed the button to answer the phone. "Hello, Mina. Yes, I'm out near the workshop with my boomerang. You made me a picnic lunch? Oh, Mina. You're the best! I'll come and get it right away. Thanks"

Susan turned back to Bodkin. "That's terrific! Mina made me a picnic lunch. I'll run up to the house, get it, and bring it back here. Then we can share lunch together. Mina is so wonderful. She always seems to know just the right thing to do."

Susan ran up to the big house and within three

minutes was back carrying a basket.

"C'mon, there's a picnic table over here. It's around the side of the workshop, but we can still see the door from there."

Susan placed the basket on the table and started to spread out the lunch.

"Oh, look what Mina did."

When they opened the basket, they discovered that Mina had carefully sliced everything in two. It was almost as if she knew that Susan had a guest. Sometimes, Susan thought that Mina was psychic.

"We have similar fruits," said Bodkin, as she popped an apple slice in her mouth, "but they're not quite the same." The next thing that she sampled was a celery stick with peanut butter, and as she started to say how much she liked it, the peanut butter got stuck to the roof of her mouth and everything she tried to say came out garbled.

Susan couldn't help giggling at her dilemma, and Bodkin quickly got caught up in the laughter. Within a minute, they were both laughing so hard that their sides hurt. Once they finally calmed down, they quickly finished the delicious lunch and put the empty containers back into the basket.

"Is Mina your grandmother?" asked Bodkin while they were cleaning up after lunch. "You seem very close."

"No, my real grandmother died almost two years ago. Mina was her nurse for the last year before she died. Then she just stayed on as Grandfather's housekeeper. She is the kindest and sweetest person I've ever met. She's become part of the family, and we love her. I still miss my grandmother, but having Mina here helps."

After finishing their lunch, Susan and Bodkin started to walk back across the yard when a bundle of black and white fur came towards them at a run. Cookie, grandfather's border collie, had spotted them.

Mina must have left the dog out after she brought out lunch.

"Stand still," said Susan. She didn't know what the dog would do. Cookie was usually friendly and she loved being out with Susan, but this was her yard and she protected it. The tiny elf girl was a stranger that she had never seen before.

When Cookie saw Bodkin, she stopped and approached slowly. Susan wasn't sure if she could grab Cookie's collar fast enough if the dog decided that she didn't like this strange person in her yard. Cookie was a herding dog and she was used to chasing unwanted guests out of her territory.

Bodkin stayed calm and still as she extended her hand carefully. A tiny blue spark jumped from Bodkin's fingertip to Cookie's nose. Cookie eyes lit up. She instantly sat down and started wagging her tail. Bodkin came up alongside Cookie, scratched her head, and whispered in her ear. They had become instant friends.

Bodkin looked over at Susan. "She is such a beautiful creature. Does she have a name?"

"Yes, she's called Cookie," answered Susan. "What did you do to her? I saw a spark jump from your finger to her nose. She's usually friendly, but she can be very protective of her yard."

"I would never harm her." said Bodkin, playfully scratching Cookie's ears. "That was just a tiny bit of magic to let her know that I was a friend. I think she likes magic."

"That was something that I wanted to ask. How are you able to do magic?"

"All elven folk have some magic in them," responded Bodkin. "With a little training, any one of us can learn a few simple tricks that have been passed down over the years. Sadly, most knowledge of magic's use has been lost. My brother, Pen, told me that years ago, when a child was found to possess a strong tendency toward magic, they would be sent to study at the Hall of Conjurers. Then the hall was destroyed and most of the guild members were killed in the Gremlin Wars. Using and controlling powerful magic requires years of practice and study. Very few still know how to use strong magic, and there's no one left to train anyone new."

"That's really sad," Susan said. "But that's not exactly what I meant when I asked. I wanted to know how you do magic."

Bodkin looked at her curiously. "Don't you know? You did manage to open the Gnome Door.

"Yes, but I don't know how I did it. When I said the word, nothing seemed to happen. Somehow I opened it by accident."

"Well, what kind of talisman were you using?" asked Bodkin.

"I wasn't using anything. I don't even know what a talisman is," said Susan.

"A talisman is a charm or an object that allows you to focus the magic. Something like this."

Bodkin reached inside her tunic and brought out a silver chain that she wore around her neck. On the end of the chain was a small chip of yellow stone in a silver setting.

"This is a tiny piece of amberstone," explained Bodkin. "No one really knows where it comes from, but it's a special type of stone that allows me to focus the magic."

Susan instantly recognized the stone. "My grandfather has a stone like that in his office."

Surprise showed on Bodkin's face. "Your grandfather has a piece of amberstone like this?"

"Not exactly like that piece," answered Susan. "There is a table in my grandfather's office with a collection of polished stones. One of the stones looks just like that, its light yellow and about the size of an egg."

Bodkin's eyes opened wide in disbelief. "Your grandfather has a completely intact amberstone? Only two whole amberstones are believed to still exist. Princess Ashley has one locked away at her castle, Kestriana. The legend is that the necromancer Eldred had a second one, and after he created the Barrier, he hid it so the wall could never be destroyed and the creatures would never escape their prison. No one has ever found it. Eldred vanished years ago and has never returned. All the remaining amberstones were thought to have been shattered in the Gremlin War. The only thing left of them are tiny pieces like mine."

"Well, I don't know where it came from," said Susan. "But it doesn't seem very special. It's not hidden or locked in a cabinet. Anyone could come and just take it."

Bodkin smiled. "Your grandfather is clever. He must have it protected in some way. It's probably surrounded by a spell that prevents it from being removed. And if it's mixed in with a bunch of polished stones, no one will even look at it twice. Hide it in plain sight. That must be how you were able to open the door."

"But I wasn't touching the stone," Susan said.

"The bigger the stone, the more powerful it is. A whole amberstone is very strong. You have touched it in the past. Usually, it takes a little while for a talisman to adjust to a new user. You must have some magic ability in you, probably from your grandfather. Magic skills are often passed down through families. You must have been close enough for the magic in your words to activate the stone, but far enough away that it took a moment for the door to open."

Susan smiled mischievously. "Well, we could go in and I'll try to open the door again. Then we'll see if it really is an amberstone."

Bodkin grinned. "We will have to be very careful, but okay. Race you to the workshop!" Bodkin took off at a run.

"No fair, wait for me," shouted Susan, as she ran to catch up with Bodkin.

As soon as they walked into the workshop, Bodkin grabbed Susan's arm and pulled her down, out of sight, motioning for her to be quiet.

Standing next to the workbench in the middle of the shop was a large, strange looking creature. It looked, to Susan, like someone had tried to cross a gorilla with a lizard. Most of its greyish-colored skin was smooth and slimy like a reptile, but there was a ridge of greasy black hair running down the middle of its back. Its head was almost flat, and it had arms that seemed too long and legs that seemed too short. It was the ugliest thing that Susan had ever seen.

Susan whispered to Bodkin "What is that thing? Ugh, it smells like rotten fruit."

Bodkin shivered "I think it's a mudwump. I've heard of them, but I've never seen one before. They normally live in the swamps, so I don't know how one could have found his way here. They're not really evil, but they can be dangerous. They're really strong and they can do a lot of damage. We can't let it get loose in your world."

"But how did it get through your spell on the other side?"

"It wasn't a very strong spell," said Bodkin. "These creatures aren't very smart, but they're attracted to magic like some birds are attracted to shiny objects. It must have sensed the magic and just went towards it. Once it got close enough, my spell wasn't strong enough to stop him. We have to get it to go back through the portal."

"But how can we do that?" asked Susan. "It's huge."

Bodkin grinned. "We should be able to trick it. Like I said, they're not that bright. If I distract it, you can sneak past it, grab the amberstone and use a little magic to lure him back through the Gnome Door."

Susan wasn't sure that she liked that plan. "But, I don't even know if I can get the stone to work for me. I've never used magic."

"You must have some magic in you. You were able to open the door. Trust your feelings, and the magic will come. That's what I was taught. You can do it."

Before Susan had a chance to argue, Bodkin took off at a run toward the mudwump. She came in from the side and slightly behind the monster where it couldn't see her. As she approached the creature, she whirled her staff high over her head and brought it down hard on the monster's big toe. The mudwump howled loudly and reached down, but Bodkin was already gone, racing across the room in the other direction and luring the creature away from Susan.

Quick as a flash, Bodkin circled behind the creature, then leaped from the floor to a cabinet and then up onto the big saw. She ran across the saw and used her staff to vault high onto the monster's shoulder. Bodkin spun her staff like a pinwheel and whacked the creature next to what looked kind of like an ear. Then she slid down the creature's back, using the monster's own hair to slow herself down as she reached the floor.

Bodkin was the bravest person that Susan had ever seen.

As the mudwump reached up to swat at its ear, it turned its back on Susan and she saw her chance. She dashed across the room toward Grandfather's office and the table with the polished stones. It only took her a second to find the plain yellow stone that she knew must be the magic amberstone. Susan grabbed the stone and turned around just in time to see the creature catch Bodkin with a huge swipe of its arm. The blow knocked Bodkin clear across the room, and she hit the wall with a terrible crash. Susan watched in horror as Bodkin slumped down onto the floor. The mudwump turned and started to shuffle slowly toward the helpless Bodkin.

"Bodkin, get up, run!" screamed Susan. But the elf girl didn't move as the monster came towards her.

"Leave her alone!" Susan yelled at the mudwump, and just as the words were leaving her mouth, a bolt of red light flew from her hand and hit the creature square in the back.

She had used the magic! Susan didn't know how she had made it work, but somehow she did. The magic bolt surprised the creature, made him stumble forward, and singed some of the hair down its back. Otherwise, it didn't seem to hurt him and he slowly turned back towards Susan. She had succeeded in getting the monster to leave Bodkin alone, but now it was coming directly at her.

Susan pointed her hand with the stone in it at the monster and nothing happened! The magic wouldn't work a second time. No matter how hard she tried or how much she wished for it, the stone stayed dull and lifeless as the monster slowly kept coming towards her.

Suddenly the creature stopped and began to swat at its face, as if it was trying to brush away a pesky insect. Wysp! Out of nowhere, the little sprite had appeared and was trying to help her. Again and again, Wysp flew into the face of the monster.

Susan had to find a way to make the magic work again. There had to be something that she was forgetting. Suddenly she thought of something that her grandfather had said, and she knew how she could make it work.

"Wysp, get out of the way!" cried Susan. As soon as the little sprite flew off, she pointed her hand at the creature, took a deep breath, and concentrated on what she knew she had to do.

As she raised her hand, the stone started to glow. A brightly colored bubble emerged from the stone. It quickly began to grow and surround the mudwump. Within seconds, the monster was completely encased within the sphere. Once inside, the creature pounded on the sides, but all of his strength just bounced harmlessly off the skin of the bubble and he was unable to escape or do any damage.

With the mudwump trapped, Susan raced over to check on Bodkin who was still crumpled in a heap on the floor.

"Oh, Bodkin, please tell me that you're okay," pleaded Susan.

But Bodkin still didn't move.

Susan started to cry. "Wysp, we have to help her,

but I don't know how to use the magic to make her wake up." She opened her hand and pleaded with the stone. "Please let me use the magic to help Bodkin." But the stone remained dull and silent.

Susan didn't know what else to do when she saw a strange blue light coming from under the workshop door. The door suddenly opened by itself, and her grandfather was there. The blue light was coming from her grandfather's carved walking stick. The carvings were glowing.

"Oh, Grandfather, I'm so sorry that I went into your shop without permission," cried Susan. "I know I've messed everything up, but Bodkin's hurt. Please help her. She's my new best friend. You can't let her die."

Grandfather moved quickly across the room and placed his hand on Bodkin's cheek.

"All right, Susan, don't cry," said Grandfather, calmly. "Move aside and I'll help her."

The blue light from the walking stick surrounded Bodkin and slowly got brighter and brighter until Susan had to look away. Grandfather never blinked, and after a minute, the light started to dim. When the light had faded enough that Susan could look again, she saw Bodkin's chest move. She was breathing. Bodkin was alive!

Grandfather put his hand on Susan's shoulder and said, "Give her a minute to recover her strength. She'll be fine soon, but she's still a little groggy."

Bodkin's eyes opened. She looked at Susan and gave her a feeble smile. "I guess I should have dodged to the left instead of the right." Then she looked up at Susan's grandfather and in a weak voice said, "Hail, Guardian."

"Hail, young Warden. I expect that you will have a large bump on the back of your head for the next few days," said Susan's grandfather as he smiled at her. "When you're feeling better, remember to thank Wysp for coming to find me on her way back here. Now please be still and rest for a few moments while I remove this creature. Susan, place that stone in Bodkin's hand and hold it there. It'll help her recover."

Susan gently put the stone in Bodkin's hand, and it instantly began to softly glow with the same blue light as her grandfather's staff.

Grandfather stood up and approached the bubble containing the confused mudwump.

He carefully laid his hand on the outside of the bubble and examined it thoroughly before asking, "Susan, did you make this?"

"Yes," Susan answered. "I was able to get the monster to leave Bodkin alone with the flash of red light, but then I couldn't get the magic to work again."

Bodkin's eyes went wide and she whispered, "Red magic."

Grandfather gave Bodkin a stern look. "Hush, Warden. Go on, Susan."

"Then I remembered something that you told me," said Susan.

"And what was it that I said?" asked Grandfather. "I'm sure that we've never talked about giant bubbles."

"Well, after the mudwump hurt Bodkin, I was so mad that I wanted to blow it into a million tiny pieces. But the stone wouldn't do anything. Then I remembered that you said that the magic couldn't be used to kill or harm things. So I thought that if I put the monster inside a big silly looking bubble, it wouldn't hurt him but it would stop him from hurting anyone else."

Grandfather smiled. "That was extremely clever, Susan. I'm very proud of you. Now, let's see what we can do about our big ugly friend here."

The carvings started to glow blue again as grandfather passed the end of his staff right through the side of the bubble without breaking it. He touched the creature with the tip of his staff. The mudwump instantly started to fade, and within a minute, Susan could see right through him. Then, an instant later, the monster was gone and Susan's brightly-colored prison popped like an ordinary soap bubble.

"But what happened to it?" asked Susan. "You said that I couldn't destroy living things with magic."

"That's correct. I didn't hurt him at all. I just sent him back to the swamp that he came from, and I made him forget how he got here so he won't be able to find his way back." Grandfather turned back toward Bodkin. "Now, young Warden in training, I believe that it's time that you were getting back to your world."

Grandfather glanced over his shoulder and said the word "traveler." As he turned back toward Bodkin, the Gnome Door began to slowly grow.

Grandfather looked over at Susan and smiled. "Don't worry, Susan, Bodkin can come back and visit soon. But right now, she needs to go home. Her brother will be worried and looking for her. Wysp has already gone on ahead to tell him that we're coming and not to worry."

Grandfather gently picked Bodkin up in spite of her claiming that she was fine, and by the time he turned back toward the door, it had grown to full size and was slowly starting to open.

As they walked toward the Gnome Door, Grandfather looked down at Susan and said. "Tomorrow, you and I have to sit down and have a long talk about magic and amberstones and lots of other stuff."

Chapter 2

That night, after Susan's adventure with Bodkin and the mudwump, her grandfather called her mother and they talked for a long time. After breakfast the next morning, Grandfather asked Susan to come to his office where they could talk about the Gnome Door. He told her that her mom had always wanted to tell her about the Gnome Door herself and had planned to do it once Susan was a little older. She wanted to apologize for all the times that she told Susan that it wasn't real, but she thought that Susan would be safer that way. Grandfather pointed out that their experience with the mudwump showed that her mother's concerns were justified. Although her mother still wanted to tell her about the world of Tir-Na-Fey herself, now that Susan knew it existed, her grandfather had permission to tell her as much as he felt that she needed to know to keep her safe. Her mom promised to come home very soon to talk to her about it, and she also agreed to let Bodkin come visit as long as her grandfather was home. After sharing their adventure with the mudwump, Susan and Bodkin quickly became best friends. They had talked about visiting the Golden Willow and, with her grandfather's help, they had finally convinced her mom to agree to the trip.

Now, here Susan was, packed and ready to go and see a whole different world. She could barely contain her excitement.

Susan wondered what it would be like to be in Bodkin's world. All the times when Bodkin had come to visit, she was tiny, the size of a doll. Would Susan and her grandfather be giants in that world? Grandfather was being very secretive and had only said that she shouldn't worry about it. "If you're finally done repacking that bag, we can get going," Grandfather said, standing in the doorway. "It's a little early, but I know you're anxious to get started."

"Oh, I'm ready," Susan said. She almost knocked Mina over as she swung her backpack off the bed. Mina somehow managed a quick sidestep to get out of the way. For someone with a bad leg, Mina sometimes moved very fast.

"Oh, Mina, I'm so sorry I almost hit you. I'm just so excited to be going."

Mina nodded. "I know, it's all right dear. No harm done. Now give me a big hug and promise me that you'll be careful. You keep an eye on your grandfather. Don't let him get into any mischief."

Susan laughed as she hugged Mina. "I absolutely promise."

Mina gave Susan's grandfather a gentle hug before turning her sternest look on him. "And you, Sir. You keep Susan safe or you will answer to me."

Grandfather mimicked Susan's answer, "I absolutely promise."

Mina shooed them out the door. "Go on then, get moving. I've got a good book, a comfy recliner chair, and the promise of three days of peace and quiet. I'm ready to get started. Don't make an old lady chase you out with a broom."

Mina walked with them out to the back porch where Susan retrieved the new walking staff that her grandfather had made for her. It was made of a very smooth white wood, and it felt good in her hand. She loved the fact that it was lightweight but very strong, and it was just the right size for her. Grandfather, as always, had his carved walking stick.

After one last hug and a scratch behind the ears for Cookie, Grandfather's border collie, they headed out across the yard.

As soon as they saw Mina go back inside the house, they turned and headed toward the workshop, to the Gnome Door. Susan didn't like the idea of hiding things from Mina, but she couldn't imagine how she could tell her that her new friend lived in a different world on the other side of a magic door. Grandfather had told Mina that they were going on a hiking trip and that Bodkin and her brother were going to meet them on the trail. All of that was true, but he left out exactly where it was that they were going hiking.

"Grandfather, can I ask you something?" Susan said as they were on their way out to the workshop. "Why is it called a Gnome Door if it takes us to the kingdom of the elves?"

"I was wondering when you would ask that," answered her grandfather with a chuckle. "The door was built by the gnomes, and a few of them still use it occasionally. The elves have their fair share of artisans and craftsmen, but they're forest people at heart. The gnomes are the master builders, masons, and architects. Building is an integral part of their culture. Gnomes used to travel everywhere, building incredible castles and whole cities. Because of that, they have established a special relationship with the spirits that dwell within the fairy mists. When I built the workshop many years ago, there was a portal in the woods nearby. The locals thought that the woods were haunted. It's one of the reasons that I moved here. Once the building was done, the gnomes came and, using special materials infused with magic, they built the door for me," said Grandfather as he opened the workshop door. "When they finished, the spirits moved the portal to where the door is now."

The Gnome Door was on the wall in Grandfather's workshop. It didn't look like anything special, just a little pretend door with an inscription written in a strange language over the top. But when the words were spoken, the door would grow to full size and open into a whole different world.

Her grandfather had taught her how to read the script years ago, and even though Susan knew the inscription by heart, she always read it silently whenever she saw the door: "Say the word 'traveler,' and the portal shall open."

As they approached the door, Grandfather asked. "Would you like to open the door for us?"

Susan nodded. She had been hoping that Grandfather would let her open the door. Since discovering that the door was real, Grandfather had been teaching her how to use magic, but she was still just a beginner.

Susan reached inside her shirt and pulled out the pendant that she wore around her neck. Tucked inside the pendant was a tiny piece of amberstone, which was a talisman that allowed her to focus the magic. When she captured the mudwump, Susan had used a fully intact amberstone which was far more powerful than the tiny sliver in her pendant. She took a deep breath, concentrated on the door, and said, "Traveler."

Nothing happened for the first few seconds, and Susan wasn't sure that it had worked until the door started to shimmer and then began to grow. Even though she had seen it a few times before, it still took her breath away when the magic happened right in front of her.

It took a moment for the door to grow to full size. As the door swung open, she could see Bodkin and her brother, Pen, waiting on the other side.

Grandfather took her hand. "Are you ready?"

Susan nodded.

"Okay then, let's go." They stepped through the door together.

A mild tingle ran down through her fingers and toes and then back up again when she stepped into the doorway. Then they were through and on the other side.

Susan glanced back over her shoulder and saw that now they were standing in front of a small cave entrance in the side of the hill.

As the two elves approached, Susan realized that both Bodkin and her brother were normal human size.

"But...you're not tiny."

Bodkin was grinning. "Yes, it's a little secret that we've been keeping until we had the chance to surprise you. Part of the magic of the door is the ability to make us small when we pass through into your world. We don't have to do that. We can remain normal size if we wish, but it makes it much easier to move around without being seen if we're tiny."

Pen embraced Grandfather. "Hail, Guardian. It is always good to see you. Are you sure that you're prepared to deal with these two for two days on your own?"

Grandfather laughed as he clasped Pen's hand. Despite the age difference, the two men genuinely liked each other. "I think I'm ready. Is Bodkin ready to go?"

"More than ready, my friend. She has spoken of nothing else for the last two days. Please, take her away and give me some solitude."

"Our housekeeper, Mina, said the same thing about Susan. You don't mind being here alone?"

"Two of my fellow wardens return every third day to make sure that the portal is well guarded, so I will have some company."

"Excellent. It should be an enjoyable two days if it doesn't rain."

"None is expected for a week. If you maintain a good pace, you should be able to easily make it to the Golden Willow by late afternoon. Tonight is the full moon and it should be a clear night. If you're lucky, you may get to see the wood fairies dance."

"Wonderful! It's been many years since I've seen them dance. That is something that everyone should get to see at least once. The girls will be ecstatic if we are lucky enough to watch that. So you know, we will be following the road north to Mistral Mountain, then turning west toward the glade of the Golden Willow. There shouldn't be many travelers on that road this time of year, and I'd prefer to remain as inconspicuous as possible. Girls, if you're ready, we can get started."

Both Susan and Bodkin responded, "We're ready."

"Then we're off. Goodbye, Pen. We'll see you in two days."

And with that, the guardian and his two young charges started off into the trees.

The two girls talked non-stop for the first hour as they walked while Grandfather followed quietly behind. Both girls had been hiking before, and they quickly fell into a nice, steady rhythm. Most of their path so far had been under the forest canopy until, almost without warning, the road opened up onto a large glen.

The three travelers had just started across the open ground when a small group of figures appeared out of the trees at the edge of the glade. They all wore cloaks and their hoods were pulled up, concealing their faces. They fanned out in a semi-circle in front of Bodkin, Susan, and her grandfather. Grandfather's staff was starting to glow blue as he said, "Girls, please move behind me."

One of the hooded figures stepped forward and raised his hand in a salute.

"Hail, Guardian. We mean you no harm, but we would like to speak with you."

Grandfather took a step toward the man and seemed to recognize him. "Korin, is that you?"

The figure drew back his hood to reveal a weathered elven face. "Your ears are still sharp, Guardian. It has been many years."

The glow of Grandfather's staff faded. "Relax, girls. Korin is an old friend."

Susan glanced over at Bodkin. Even though she was behind Grandfather's protective staff, Bodkin had an arrow drawn back on her bow and it was pointed directly at Korin the elf.

"Bodkin, please lower your bow," said Susan's grandfather. Bodkin did as she was asked but eyed the group suspiciously and kept the arrow ready.

"Korin, you, of all people know that I am no threat to the elves. Why would you approach in such a manner?"

"My apologies, old friend, but it was necessary. As I stated, one of us would speak with you."

From the center of the group, one of the figures stepped forward and lowered her hood. Golden hair cascaded down across her shoulders.

Bodkin gasped out loud, and Grandfather said, "Susan, stand up straight."

"Please, allow me, Guardian," the figure said as she extended a delicate hand toward Susan. The woman was tall and beautiful, with only a few small age lines showing on her otherwise finely chiseled features.

"Hello, Susan, I'm Princess Ashley. I've heard much about you."

Susan stepped forward and took the princess's hand. "I'm very pleased to meet you, Your Highness, I mean, Princess, I mean...oh, I'm sorry, I don't know what to call you."

The Princess laughed. Her laughter was pleasant and soothing, like water tumbling over rocks.

"Why don't you just call me 'Ashley'?"

Susan shook her head. "No, I'm sorry. I don't mean to be rude, but Mom says that it's impolite to call adults by their first name. Would just 'Princess' be okay?"

The princess smiled warmly. "Of course. Your mother is right. 'Princess' it is then."

Susan glanced over to see that Bodkin had dropped to one knee when the princess revealed her identity.

The princess turned slightly. "Rise, young Bodkin. We have also heard of your bravery. A mudwump can be a very formidable opponent."

Bodkin looked surprised. "But...I told no one."

The princess smiled at her. "Except your brother, Pen, whose duty as a warden of the forest requires him to report anything as serious as a creature like the mudwump passing through into the other world. The two of you had quite an adventure. Please don't be angry with your brother. He reported it only to me, and I was already aware of what had happened. The sprite, Wysp, is a bit of a blabbermouth. She told me the whole story before Pen had the chance to report it, although Wysp's version had her single-handedly saving the two of you. I do believe that Pen's telling of the story was a bit more accurate. Bodkin, please come and stand before me."

Bodkin stepped forward and stood directly in front of Princess Ashley.

The princess stood up very straight, put her hand on Bodkin's shoulder, and addressed her formally.

"Bodkin, as your princess, I commend your courage, but I also need your promise that you will not attempt anything so dangerous again. At least not until you have had further training. If the guardian had not arrived when he did, your adventure could have ended very badly, and we cannot afford to lose such a promising young warden."

Bodkin was beaming. "I swear it, My Lady."

Princess Ashley smiled broadly. "Excellent, Thank you, Bodkin. Now, I would like to speak privately with Cooper."

Susan and Bodkin both looked at each other and said, "Cooper?"

The expressions of both the Princess and Korin showed their amusement. Princess Ashley said, "Your grandfather didn't tell you that before he became a guardian, he was just called Cooper."

Princess Ashley looked toward Grandfather. "Well, Guardian, it seems that you have a story to tell these girls while you travel."

The princess knelt down so she could address the two girls directly.

"Susan, I need to borrow your grandfather for a few minutes, please, if you and Bodkin would relax here for a short time. Korin and his men will keep you safe, and we will not be long."

"I don't need them to keep me safe," Bodkin whispered under her breath.

"Well then, perhaps you can keep us safe," said Korin with a smile.

Princess Ashley took Grandfather's arm and started toward the far side of the clearing. Susan noticed that there was something familiar about the way the princess held her grandfather's arm and walked with him. It reminded her of her grandmother.

Far above a lone falcon circled slowly. They were almost to the far side of the glade before either one spoke.

"The silver in your hair suits you, Cooper."

"Thank you, I've been told that it helps to rinse it in a tankard of ale from time to time."

The princess couldn't resist giggling at that remark. "And your wit is still sharp. It is good to see you again."

"The years have also been kind to you, Princess. You are still as lovely as you were that first night that we met. But I didn't come to chat with old acquaintances. I have only come so that Susan can spend a few quiet days with her new friend. I won't waste time asking you how you knew that we would be here. What I do want to know, though, is what could be so important that you would risk the king's anger to come here in secret and talk to me?"

"It concerns Prax! Coramina has heard his thoughts."

"The dragon is still alive? How can that be after all this time? No one has seen him for over forty years. His injuries were so severe after his battle with the lindworm that he could barely fly. Everyone thought that he just went off to die. We searched for him many times. No trace of him was ever found."

"Yes, all that is true. It is also true that dragons sometimes disappear for years at a time. Forty years is a very long time, but Cora believes that she has heard his voice in her dreams. He keeps asking for someone to come and release him. She is certain that the voice she hears *is* the dragon, Prax, and that he is trapped somewhere."

"And I suppose, you want me to find him for you, don't you? You give me an impossible choice, Ashley. You know that I owe a great debt to Prax. My wife would have died if not for him. And I have no doubt that both girls would jump at the chance to go searching for the dragon, but I swore to Susan's mother that I would keep her safe. That was the only way that she would allow Susan to come here. My daughter, Elana, knows of some of the dangers in your world. I cannot risk Susan's safety on a wild dragon hunt."

"There shouldn't be any risk. Cora believes that Prax is located somewhere near the base of Mistral Mountain. Your trip is to see the Golden Willow. You will pass right by the mountain along the way. A quick search would not pose any danger. If you should be able to find him and he is trapped somehow, I can send men to try and free him."

"Princess, I've been away for a long time, but not long enough that I can be fooled that easily. That talkative Wysp told you about the amberstone and now you want me to have Susan use the red magic to search for the dragon."

"But if Prax still lives, we *must* try to find him. He deserves that much. And you have an intact amberstone! The one that Eldred was supposed to have hidden, no doubt. I should be furious that you've kept that little secret from me for all these years."

"This is exactly the reason that I have kept it hidden. Its use attracts evil. You have your own amberstone, and *you* are also able to use the red magic, Princess. Why not just search for the dragon yourself?"

"I would gladly do that. I also owe much to the dragon, but as you well know, there is no Guild of Conjurors anymore, and any use of the one remaining amberstone would have to be approved by the High Council. The stone is locked in a vault and protected by both guards and magic. Of course, getting the High Council to agree on anything is next to impossible."

Cooper snickered. "Politicians are the same everywhere."

"I also believe that there is someone on the council who would like to see both my father and I removed from power. I don't know who it is yet, but someone is working to undermine everything we do."

"Some things never change, Princess."

"This is more than the standard court intrigue, Cooper. I believe that there is a source of evil as great as the one we fought against in the Gremlin War and a member of the High Council is their puppet. We suspect that they may even try to destroy the Barrier."

Cooper looked skeptical. "Do you have anything to base this belief on?"

"Cora has sensed a great evil, but she cannot find the source. Some members of the council are very skilled at hiding their thoughts."

Cooper sighed. "All right, Ashley. Coramina is not usually prone to exaggeration. When we get to the base of Mistral Mountain, I will attempt a short search. But at the first sign of any danger, I will take Susan and return home whether we find any trace of Prax or not. Agreed?"

"Agreed! Thank you, Cooper." Ashley kissed him on the cheek.

"You're welcome, and please refrain from doing that in front of Susan and Bodkin. We don't want them getting the wrong impression. Now, let's get back to the group so the girls and I can be on our way."

"Very well. Would you at least walk slowly so that I may enjoy an extra few minutes with you? I so rarely find time to reminisce with old friends, and I remember that you did care for me once." The Princess took his arm once again as they started back to where the girls and Ashley's guards waited. A silent shadow passed over the clearing. Suddenly the quiet of the glade was shattered by the shrill cry of the falcon.

The bird shrieked as it dove straight toward the princess. Its talons were extended, as if it meant to tear her eyes out. The princess tried to duck, and the guardian's staff flared with blue light. The bird was only inches from the princess, but an instant before it could strike, the falcon suddenly veered off wildly and landed in the grass where it flopped once and then lay still. There was an arrow through the bird's throat. All eyes turned to see Bodkin poised with her bow in case another bird appeared.

Instantly, weapons appeared in the hands of Korin and his men. Even the princess held a long dagger. When no further attack came, the princess spoke quietly. "Cooper, can the bird tell us anything useful?"

Cooper's staff lit up as the blue light reached out toward the dead bird. The instant the light touched the bird's feathers, the corpse ignited in green flames. In seconds, all that remained was a foul smelling lump of black slime.

Cooper's tone was harsh and angry. "It was definitely bewitched. Return to your castle, Ashley. I will not allow the girls to be put in danger because of your petty court intrigues and power struggles. Leave us in peace. Susan, Bodkin, pick up your gear, please. We're leaving. Goodbye, Princess."

Grandfather turned on his heel and strode across the glade as the two girls scrambled to keep up.

"Damn that little elf girl and her bow," Shirell cursed under her breath. Not only had she lost a valuable spy in her falcon, but she had failed in her attempt to blind Princess Ashley. She knew that she would almost certainly lose the bird when she decided to use it to attack the princess, but she had hoped that it would at least accomplish its task, even if it didn't escape.

Blinding the princess would have thrown both the royal house and the Elven High Council into turmoil. Instead, all that Shirell had succeeded in doing was to confirm the princess's suspicions that she possessed a serious enemy and needed to be extra careful. Fortunately, few believed that witches existed anymore. The princess's protectors would be looking for a male magic-wielder, a rogue wizard. Still, she couldn't allow herself to get careless.

Spying on the elves had just become a lot more difficult. She would need to find a new familiar. Shirell could easily follow the elves back to their city and move about freely, but with her raven hair and dark eyes, she stood out. She would be noticed anywhere she went in a community of fair-skinned elves.

The bird had been an excellent choice for a spy. No one gave a second glance to a falcon circling overhead. That's what they do naturally. Now, the princess and her guards would be looking up, wary of another attack. Shirell needed someone lower to the ground. Someone like Pinkie.

Pinkie was a snicker, a small squirrel-like creature with reddish brown fur. The name snicker came from the sounds they made if something surprised or startled them. It was common to find a snicker sunning itself on a low hanging branch or scurrying across a rooftop ridge. No one would pay much attention to a playful snicker sitting on the window ledge.

An hour after their encounter with the princess, the three stopped for a short rest. Grandfather had calmed down and was back to his usual self.

Susan sat down next to him on a stump. "You don't like the princess very much, do you?"

"I'm sorry if I got angry, Susan. Actually, I like the princess a lot. Before I met your grandmother, we were very close."

"Were you in love with her?"

"That's a question that we'll save until you're a little older. I have great respect for the princess. She's an excellent ruler. Fair and honest. She loves the elven people more than anything else in the world. She can be kind and gentle, but she's also one of the bravest and fiercest fighters I've ever known. There is no one that I would rather have protecting my back if I would have to go into battle."

"So why did you get so mad at her?"

"Princess Ashley attracts trouble. A lot of that isn't her fault. Anyone in a position of power, sooner or later, gains enemies. She doesn't look for trouble, but it always seems to find her. And people close to Ashley tend to get hurt. I don't want either you or Bodkin put in danger unnecessarily."

"What did she want to talk to you about?"

Grandfather sighed. "Bodkin, could you come over here please?" Once Bodkin was within hearing distance, he said "The Princess would like us to search for the dragon, Prax."

Susan's face lit up. "Search for a dragon? Really? Oh, Grandfather, can we do it? Please?"

Bodkin was clearly skeptical. "But the rumors about Prax still being alive somewhere are just legends. He flew off to die after defeating the lindworm at the end of the war. Pen told me that story many times when we were young."

"No one really knows exactly what happened to him. I was there. He destroyed the lindworm and devastated the Gremlin Army, but he was badly injured. When it was clear that the elves had won, he just turned and flew off. After many years, when he never returned, everyone believed that he must have died. But dragons are very hard to kill, and they sometimes disappear for years at a time. The Court Psychic Lady Coramina believes that she has heard him calling out to her in her dreams. Our path takes us right past the base of the Mistral Mountain. That's where she believes he may be."

"So, are we going to do it?" Susan could barely contain her excitement.

"I agreed to conduct a quick search only because it will allow you to practice a little magic. If we should happen to find any sign of Prax, or if, as I suspect, we don't find anything, we'll send a message to the princess and then continue on our way. But for now, we should keep moving or we won't have any time for a search." They walked in silence for a while until Susan's curiosity finally got the better of her.

"Grandfather, why does the princess call you 'Cooper?'"

Grandfather chuckled. "I was wondering how long it would take you to bring that up. It's nothing bad. It's more of a title than a name. A cooper is someone who makes barrels and kegs. When my grandfather was a young man in Ireland, he was trained as a carpenter, cabinet maker, and cooper. When he came to America, he got a job working for a brewer, and when I was just about your age, he started to teach me.

"After I finished school a few years later, my friend, John, and I decided to hike across Europe for a few months. See the world before looking for some boring nine to five job. We would stop in small towns, stay for a short time, and then continue on to another town. The skills that my grandfather taught me allowed us to earn a little money to support ourselves while we traveled. It was a lot of fun and a great experience. We met a lot of charming people in those small towns.

"Well...in this one little village, we found a winemaker who needed some new casks. The job didn't pay us very much because he only needed a few, but he said that he was impressed with our work and he could recommend us to two men that needed quite a few barrels. We were almost out of money, so we said that we'd take the job.

"The winemaker set up a meeting with the two men at the local pub. They were two brothers, Quark and

Quisp. The brothers weren't really much older than we were, and they were very friendly. We haggled back and forth for a while before settling on a fair price, and they agreed to hire us. Once the business talk was out of the way, we stayed and talked and laughed until late into the night. We all got very drunk.

"When John and I woke up the next day, we were at an inn in a small village that neither of us had ever seen before. We couldn't remember how we got there. The town looked very old and a little odd, but we both had such terrible headaches that we didn't care very much.

"The two brothers came by in the afternoon and took us to the workshop that they had set up for us. It was about a half mile outside of town. They had rooms upstairs above the shop where we could stay. Then later, in the afternoon, they took us to visit a blacksmith who had agreed to make the iron rings for the barrels and manufacture any tools that we might need.

"The next morning, we got started building barrels.

"It didn't take long before we started to notice some strange things about this village. It was like we had stepped back in time. There was no electric anywhere in the whole town. The shop had a big saw set up with a waterwheel, but it didn't work and the two brothers didn't know how to fix it. John had some engineering training and was pretty handy at fixing things, so within two days, we had it running and John even made some improvements to it. Most of the rest of our work had to be done with hand tools.

"The brothers had arranged for a local woman to bring us meals, but she always kept her hood pulled up so we never got a good look at her. She didn't speak to us, and she never stayed more than a moment. In our earlier travels, we found that some people in these small towns were very private and didn't like outsiders, so we didn't think too much of it and just tried to be polite anytime she came.

"The two brothers asked us not to go into town, but we were young men who enjoyed a night out from time to time. We quickly got bored and tired of hanging around the workshop every evening, so we decided to sneak into the town and see if we could find a pub and maybe have a little fun. We were sure that if we crept in near the edge of the forest, we could slip in quietly and maybe make a few new friends before anyone noticed us and threw us out.

"We made it to the outskirts of the town. I could just see the lights in some of the windows when hands came out of the dark, grabbed me, threw a dark hood over my head, tied my hands, and roughly dragged me off. John suffered the same fate. We were taken into a building and bound to chairs. After five minutes in the chairs, we heard the door open, followed by a number of loud voices. Two of the voices we recognized as belonging to the two brothers that we worked for. The hoods were removed and we were face to face with some very angry looking men who all had pointed ears. We didn't know where we were, but suddenly, we were absolutely sure that we were no longer in some little town in Europe.

"Eventually, things calmed down and we were able to piece together what was going on. We had somehow been brought into an elven village in a whole different world. Quark and Quisp ran the pub in this village and had a reputation as the town mischief makers. They weren't really bad. They just always seemed to find some way to get into trouble with the town elders. On the night that we met, they put something in our drinks and slipped us through the fairy mists during the night. There were a few small communities of humans in this world, mostly farming villages along the border, but the king had forbidden any contact."

"Why would the king do that?" asked Susan.

"Many years ago, a man from one of these villages went through one of the portals into the human world. Some of the humans still had families in our world, and it was fairly common to do that. There were no cell phones back then, and traveling was expensive, so if you told your relatives that you lived in a different country, nobody questioned it. When the farmer returned, he was sick with influenza. The elves had no resistance to the disease, and it traveled quickly. Many died. Then it spread to some of the other races. The elves blamed the humans for bringing the disease here. The gnomes blamed the elves for allowing the humans to travel back and forth through the portals. The trolls blamed the gnomes for spreading the disease as they traveled from place to place building structures, and everyone sealed themselves off in their own lands and threatened anyone crossing their borders. Finally, with the help of some human doctors, the healers of this world were able to contain the illness, but not before numerous deaths. A lot of ill will was created between the races. After a time, things calmed down and trade slowly started up again, but there are still occasional outbreaks and when that happens, the king forbids contact."

Susan was puzzled. "So why would the brothers bring you here in secret if they knew that they'd get in trouble?"

Grandfather chuckled. "Well, it had been a few years since the last outbreak, and the ban on human contact wasn't really enforced much, especially in some of the smaller villages. They did keep us away from the village long enough to be sure that we were healthy. It also seemed that the two brothers had secretly visited the human world a few times and discovered that the ale in our world was much better than theirs. Being pub owners, they wanted to find out how the ale was brewed differently to make it better. Better ale meant more customers, more customers meant more money.

"What they discovered was that their ale was brewed by almost the same method, but humans stored it in oaken kegs to let it age and gain flavor from the wood. They decided that they needed some oaken kegs."

"So couldn't they just buy some or make some of their own?"

"Well...that's where the problem was. Elves heat their homes using a special peat that grows almost everywhere, can easily be harvested and dried, and burns clean and smoke free. They have no need for firewood. Their homes are built of stone and other natural materials. They don't use lumber. Elves live at the edge of the forests and love the trees. They don't cut down trees unless they're sick or dead. Woodworking is almost unknown to the elves. There are gnomes who have some skill working with wood, but they live far to the east and there were still a lot of hard feelings toward the elves. . No one in this part of the land made barrels or even knew how to.

"Quark and Quisp thought that if they could hire a few humans, sneak them through the mists, and have them build barrels for them, they would have the only supply. They could brew the best ale in the land and sell a few barrels on the side. They would make lots of money. That rule about not having contact with humans was just a minor inconvenience to their plans."

"So what happened?"

"Well....Quark and Quisp had a lot of experience at talking their way out of trouble, and even the most stubborn of the elders enjoyed a good tankard of ale. So the two brothers managed to convince them that as long as no one knew we were here, what would it hurt? Their village was on the outskirts of the province. If everyone kept quiet, there was no real harm done. And if their plan worked, they would all get to enjoy the best ale in the area. It took some fast talking, but as long as we promised to keep a low profile, the elders agreed to let us stay for a time, at least until we found out if the brother's idea would work."

"But when you found out that you were in a whole different world, weren't you scared? Didn't you want to go home?"

"Well, the original reason for our trip was to meet new people and experience different things. Besides that, we had agreed to do the job, and that was important to us. The fact that our employers were elves didn't really change that. And we quickly discovered that people in an elven village weren't very much different from people in a human village. So we stayed and made some barrels. Quark and Quisp brewed a batch of ale and stored it in our kegs. After three months, we cracked open a cask and sampled the ale. The oak from the barrel had given it a deeper and richer flavor. The ale was definitely improved from aging in the kegs. The two brothers were overjoyed. They immediately took the open keg into the pub and offered a free glass to anyone who would sample their new ale. The brothers' pub quickly became a very popular place as word of the improved quality of their brew started to spread. Even the elders were pleased, though they were reluctant to admit it openly. It soon became common to see folks from surrounding villages, travelers and total strangers in the pub.

"One night, a small group came into the pub. There were three men and a woman. Quisp told me that they were wardens of the forest."

"Like Bodkin and Pen?"

"That's right. The men seemed to know most of the locals and stopped to talk and socialize. The woman got herself a tankard of ale and started toward the table in the corner where I was sitting alone. She was very pretty, so when she asked if she could sit down, I certainly wasn't going to say no.

"She sat down and took a drink from the mug and said, 'Well, that really is very good. So you must be the mysterious human responsible for this fine ale. What do they call you, Human?'

"The townspeople call me Cooper, although it's more of a title than a name. Sort of like blacksmith. And you are?

"'Thirsty,' she quipped. Then she took another gulp from the tankard. 'They tell me that you work with wood. That's a very unusual skill around here.'

"So I've been told. We have a workshop a half mile up the road. Would you like to see it? It's a clear night and the moon is out. It's not far.

She sat up straight and looked at me curiously. 'Did you just ask me to go for a walk in the moonlight with you?'

"Yes, I think I did. Are you coming?

She gave me a funny little smirk and said, 'That might be fun. Let's take a walk.'

"I started across the crowded pub with the girl following a step behind. When I reached the center of the floor she stopped me.

"'Oh, Cooper, just a moment.'

"As I turned around, the girl reached up and poured the entire tankard of ale over my head.

"'I'm sorry, but I've changed my mind. Maybe next time,' she said as she set the glass on a nearby table and went out the door grinning.

"The entire pub exploded with laughter as I stood there soaking wet and wondering what had just happened.

"One of the girl's companions came up behind me, put his hand on my shoulder, and said, 'Don't feel too bad, my friend. She meant it in good fun. A word of advice, though. It is considered very rude to ask an elf girl to go for a walk in the moonlight the very first time that you meet her. *And*, the princess never goes for walks in the moonlight with young men. But I think she likes you. She didn't throw you to the ground and demand an apology like she does with most young men. I'm Korin, and I promise you that we'll stop here again soon. Talk to her the next time we come, just don't ask her to go for a walk and don't let her get behind you if you do.' He gave me a friendly pat on the back and followed her out the door, laughing."

Bodkin had been listening in the whole time and both girls were giggling as she asked, "So Princess Ashley poured a glass of ale over your head the first time you met?"

"Yes, I'm afraid she did."

"And the man named Korin. Was that the same man that we met in the glade?"

"Yes, he's been one of Ashley's personal guards for many years. As soon as I saw him today, I knew that the princess had to be with him." Cooper stopped and gestured with his walking stick. "Look ahead, I think that we've reached the edge of the forest."

Chapter 3

The trees parted, and the travelers found themselves walking out onto the grassy foothills at the base of the mountain. Their impression of the mountain, now that it loomed over them, was quite different from when they had just caught glimpses through the canopy of the trees.

The face of Mistral Mountain was harsh and craggy. Sheer cliffs and steep rock formations dotted the sides of the mountain. It would take an experienced climber to try to scale it.

Bodkin looked up at it in dismay. "We don't have to climb that, do we?"

"No, our path turns west and skirts around the base of the mountain. We can just follow the edge of the trees," Cooper answered.

Susan was anxious to start the search. "What about the dragon? Where do we look for him?"

"The princess said to look for a small hill near the witch's cauldron."

Bodkin was having second thoughts about approaching the forbidding mountainside. "A cauldron? What's that supposed to mean? There haven't been any witches for a hundred years."

"Yes, Bodkin, I know. But that's the image that Lady Coramina saw. Remember, it's a dream image, so it's not going to be exact. We'll just have to look carefully."

Susan touched her grandfather's arm. "I can see a small hill this way. We could start to look there."

"An excellent idea, Susan. Come along, Bodkin."

From a distance, the hill didn't appear to be anything special. Nothing but earth, rocks and some scrub grass.

Bodkin wasn't impressed. "It's just a big pile of dirt. There's no dragon here."

They had gone about half the distance to the hill when Susan pointed up at the side of the mountain. "Look up there. At those rocks."

Fifty yards above the hill, a small ridge jutted out from the cliff face. Perched on the ridge was a boulder that was almost round with a flat spot on top. On either side of the boulder were two rock piles. It didn't require much imagination to picture a cauldron flanked by a pair of witches in the rock formation.

The two girls instantly started toward the hill when Cooper stopped them.

"Susan, I need to tell you something important before we begin to search for the dragon. Do you remember when you first met Bodkin and you tried to save her from the mudwump using my amberstone? You said that the light from the magic was red."

"Yes, I remember. The red light just made the creature stumble, but didn't really seem to hurt him."

"The ability to do red magic is very rare, only a few people can do it. Even I don't possess the gift of red magic. The red magic is very special and can do things that regular magic can't do. It can allow you to uncover other magic that's hidden. That's why Princess Ashley came to us and asked us to look for the dragon. Wysp told her that you were able to do red magic. Ashley knew that if the dragon was trapped somewhere, the entrance to his prison would be disguised and red magic might be needed to expose the hiding place. If we are going to find where the dragon is imprisoned, I will need you to try to use the red magic."

"I'll try, Grandfather, but I don't know how I did it the first time."

"Use the same method that we've practiced. Stay calm and concentrate. Focus on shining the red light on the hillside. If any other magic exists there, the red light will make it appear." Cooper reached into a hidden pocket and pulled out a dull yellow stone. "And use this."

"You brought the amberstone!" Susan took the enchanted stone and held it out in her hand. She tried to clear her mind and concentrate on what she wanted to do. So much had happened in the last few hours that it was hard to think about just one thing. She needed something to focus her thoughts on, so she thought about her grandmother. No one ever made her feel as safe and calm as her grandmother. When she thought about her grandmother's smile, all the other stuff seemed less overwhelming. Susan let that warm feeling take over her thoughts as she closed her eyes, took a deep breath, and concentrated on the red magic. When she heard Bodkin gasp, she slowly opened her eyes.

Red light was shining from her hand onto the side of the hill. Susan was so surprised that the light flickered and almost went out. But she quickly caught herself, restored the light, and then carefully started to sweep the hill with the special magic.

The red light passed over the face of the knoll as Susan slowly moved her hand from left to right. Near the center of the hill, a dark spot appeared and slowly grew to expose a cave entrance as Susan lingered on it. Once the entrance was fully revealed, she allowed the light to fade.

"Very good, Susan. I think that you've found what we were looking for," said Cooper.

Two faceless stone figures that were fifteen feet tall flanked the entrance. Each one held one arm up to the roof of the cave and appeared to be supporting the entrance. The other hand was by their side. In front of each figure stood a six-foot tall obelisk of black obsidian. In the face of each obelisk was a twelve-inch, round opening.

Bodkin instantly started toward the entrance. "C'mon, let's go."

Cooper's commanding voice froze her in her tracks. "Bodkin, *stop!*"

The elf girl was only a half-step from the entrance. She slowly inched backwards until she was back with the other two.

Cooper picked up a small twig from the ground and threw it into the entrance between the two stone giants. There was a flash of blinding light as the twig exploded into splinters.

Bodkin was clearly shaken. "A booby-trap! And I almost walked right into it. What are those things?"

"The statues are called Golem Twins, and they're alive. Even though they were created with magic, they're made of natural materials, earth and stone, so they're not affected by most magic. The twins are mirror images of each other. One is good and helpful; the other is evil and will destroy anyone who tries to pass between them."

"So how do we get past them?" Susan asked.

"They will always give you a choice. If you look there, you can see that the twins support the entrance and there are two obelisks. You must place your hand in the opening of one of the obelisks. If you pick correctly, the Golem Twins will turn back into harmless stone and the way will be clear. Pick incorrectly and they will release the ceiling, dropping tons of rock on whoever is standing before them."

"But how can you know which one is the right one?"

"We can ask one of the twins one question only. One of them will always tell the truth, the other will always lie."

Bodkin looked puzzled. "What good is that? You still don't know which one is good or bad."

"You just have to ask the right question. Stay here, please."

Cooper approached the twin on the right. "Golem, if I was to ask your companion to show me the correct obelisk, which one would he point to?"

The stone guardian slowly raised his arm and pointed to the obelisk on the left.

Bodkin was still confused. "So which one do we pick?"

"Well, Bodkin, if this is the good twin and he's telling us the truth, then his companion is the evil one who would tell us to pick the left one, knowing that it would cause our destruction. Therefore the right obelisk should be the good one. But if this is the evil twin, he knows that his partner, the good twin, will tell us which one is the correct choice. Therefore he will lie and tell us the opposite of what his twin would say. So if this is the evil twin and he's telling us to pick the one on the left, then he's lying and, once again, the one on the right is the safe one."

Cooper placed his right hand into the obelisk on the right. A bright light instantly surrounded his hand and, as the three travelers watched, the shape of the Golem Twins started to change. Their outlines started to blur and after a moment it was impossible to distinguish them from the surrounding rocks.

Grandfather turned and smiled at the two girls. "I guess that was the right question."

Before going into the cave, Cooper took off his pack, laid it on the ground, and pulled out a large flashlight. "Susan, will you get out your flashlight? We can store our gear over by the trees. Bodkin, you don't have a light, so once we get inside, I want you to take my hand so we don't get separated."

At fifty yards in, the tunnel turned to the right. Three steps after they turned the corner, Cooper stopped and had them return to the bend in the tunnel.

"Just a moment, Susan. Bodkin, I need you to go back to the entrance, get your bow, and stand guard. We won't be long."

Without a word, Bodkin immediately nodded and headed back out of the tunnel. Susan watched until she could see Bodkin silhouetted in the light of the entrance, and then she turned on her grandfather.

    "Grandfather, that was mean! Why did you make her go back? She wants to find the dragon as much as we do."

    "I know, Susan. I sent her back because she's claustrophobic. She's afraid of small, dark places. As soon as we turned the corner, she started squeezing my hand so hard that I could barely feel my fingers. She's terrified but doesn't want to admit that she's scared. Did you notice that she didn't argue or hesitate when I told her to go back?"

    "So that's why you were holding her hand? How did you know that she'd be scared?"

    "Elves love the forests. Their homes are open and airy. They're used to being outside. And things are a bit different in this world. Here, every elf child knows that there really are bad things that live in the dark places. It's unusual to find an elf that isn't claustrophobic. If someone did trap Prax, they're very clever. They know that if anyone was to come looking for the dragon, it would almost certainly be elves and that they would avoid looking in a cave. Also, you remember the falcon that tried to attack the princess. It was being controlled by someone, maybe the same someone who trapped the dragon and doesn't want anyone to find him. It is possible that we're being watched or followed. A cave is an easy place for someone to sneak up from behind and ambush you. It's a good idea to have someone guarding the exit. But now we should keep moving. We told Bodkin that we would hurry."

    Further in, the corridor opened up into a small chamber. On the far side, another corridor led off into a black void. Otherwise, the room was empty.

    "I think that we've been sent on a fool's errand, Susan. There doesn't appear to be anything here, and this cave is far too small to house a dragon as big as Prax. Wait here. I am going to explore a short distance down the other corridor. I won't go very far, so I'll still be able to hear you if you call. I won't be more than five minutes, but we shouldn't leave without at least looking in that corridor. There may be some clue to the dragon's whereabouts hidden there. Someone put those Golem Twins at the entrance for a reason."

Cooper shone his flashlight into the tunnel, and his staff started to glow as he entered. He was taking no chances that there might be something unpleasant waiting for him in the dark. Susan started to examine the small room while she waited. Perhaps there was something that they had missed in the dark. She used her flashlight to carefully scan the walls, floor, and even the ceiling. Except for a few strange looking rock formations, the chamber was completely empty.

From behind Susan, a voice like distant thunder asked, "Are you real?"

Susan jumped at the unexpected voice and spun around to see nothing but a blank rock wall. She examined the wall carefully and was just starting to wonder if she had imagined the voice when an odd shaped section of rock blinked and opened to reveal an eye the size of a soccer ball.

A dragon's eye. The dragon was not imprisoned in the cave. He was part of the cave. Susan suddenly understood why no one had seen the dragon for so many years. He had been trapped in stone.

"Are you *real*, child? You smell real, but I have been imprisoned here for so long that sometimes I can no longer tell if I am dreaming or not. Can you speak, or are you just another nightmare come to torment me?"

Susan couldn't believe it. She had not only found the dragon, but it had spoken to her and was waiting for an answer.

"No, I'm not a nightmare. I'm real," she stuttered. "I'm sorry, I didn't know that you could speak. Please believe me. I'm really here."

"You smell of both elf and human. Do you have a name, child?"

"Yes, my name is Susan, so you don't need to call me 'child.' And I'm not an elf. I'm a human from the world on the other side of the Gnome Door."

"Very well, Susan, I meant no disrespect, but I am over a thousand years old and maybe the last of my kind. To me, everyone is a child. I know of your world on the other side of the mists. Long ago, I spent a few centuries there. But you do have elf blood. My nose is never wrong. It tells me that you came here with two companions. One is an elf girl of the Tek clan. The other is a human. His scent is familiar. He fought in the Gremlin Wars. Please, tell me, what is his name?"

"Here he is called Cooper. I call him Grandfather."

"Cooper is your grandfather? How long have I been here, Susan?"

"Grandfather says that it has been forty years since anyone has seen a dragon."

"I remember this man called Cooper. The barrel maker. He was also a student of the wizard Eldred. He fought bravely with both magic and sword. He fell in love with the Princess, and she with him."

"But, you must be mistaken. After the war, he returned home to our world and married a human woman. Princess Ashley stayed here. I can't be an elf."

"Well....the Princess Ashley *was* in love with Cooper, but then, she was not the only princess."

"What!" Susan was dumbfounded. Grandfather had never mentioned a second princess.

"There was another princess. A younger sister named Anna."

"My grandmother was called Anna."

"Are you still so sure that you are not part elf? How were you able to find this cave? Did you use red magic?"

"Yes, that's right."

"Only members of the royal elven family have the ability to use red magic. Your grandmother must have been the princess."

"Enough, Dragon!" Cooper's voice boomed from the entrance of the corridor. "We have more important concerns than my love life."

Susan looked at her grandfather. "Is it true? Am I an elf? Was Grandma Anna really an elven princess?"

"Yes, Susan. The dragon is telling the truth." Cooper sighed, "Your mother asked me not to say anything. Both your mother and grandmother felt that your mother should be the one to tell you once you were old enough. She had planned to do that when we returned. Even when your grandmother was going through treatments, she always wore a silly hat so you wouldn't notice her pointed ears. I'm so sorry that we've kept secrets from you. Your mother promised me that she would explain everything to you as soon as you got home. We can talk later, but I need you to be patient a little longer while we try to help Prax. I will still need your help."

Susan's head was spinning. There was so much to think about all at once. Inside her head, she could hear Grandmother Anna's voice saying, "Sometimes, you just have to stop, count to ten, take a deep breath, and decide what's really important. Then it's easy to know what to do."

Susan took a deep breath, hugged her grandfather, and asked. "What can we do to free Prax?"

Cooper turned his attention to the dragon. "Prax, I know that dragons can feel magic and understand it better than humans. Do you know who imprisoned you here? Or how? Is there anything that you can tell us that might help break the spell that holds you here?"

"I have spent years probing the magic that holds me here. I do not know who wove this prison of magic, but I do know that it was created in layers, spell on top of spell, to make it strong enough to prevent me from breaking free. That means that there must be one weak spot, a point where all the spells originated from. The stone that the conjurer stood upon while working his magic could not be included in all the other spells and would need to be protected with one last spell. That last spell needed to be weak enough for the conjurer to escape, because as soon as it was put into place, it would complete the prison. The spell-weaver would only have seconds to escape or be trapped in here with me."

"There is a small tunnel at the other side of this chamber. It ends at a blank wall twenty yards in."

"That must have been his way out, his back door. He has since sealed the other end, but the keystone must be very near to his escape route. Find that keystone and destroy it, and I will be released."

"Susan, do you think that you can call up the red magic again?" asked Cooper.

Susan nodded as her grandfather handed her the amberstone. She closed her eyes and tried to focus her thoughts. Crimson light was shining from her hand when she opened her eyes. She directed it at the tunnel at the rear of the chamber. She let the light flow down the tunnel, but nothing appeared. She walked over to the tunnel entrance and flooded the entire tunnel with the red light. Still, nothing appeared. Susan slowly withdrew the light from the tunnel and illuminated the entrance. Still, they found nothing. Susan was becoming frustrated and the light was starting to dim.

Cooper placed his hand on her shoulder. "Just a little more, Susan. Then you can stop if you need to."

The red light was fading, and Susan didn't think that she could keep it going much longer when a spot appeared on the floor twenty feet from the tunnel entrance. The light instantly returned to full brightness as a rectangular stone set in the floor began to glow.

"That must be the stone. Susan, I need you to hold the light on that stone. Can you do that?" asked Cooper.

"Yes, I think so." It was easier to maintain the light when she had something to focus it on.

Her grandfather's staff glowed bright blue as he called up magic of his own. The blue light began to surround the red light, mixing the two magics together until the stone glowed purple. Tiny wisps of smoke snaked toward the ceiling. Purple light radiated out in all directions as the stone slowly disintegrated into dust.

As Susan allowed the light to fade, she suddenly became very light-headed and realized that Cooper's hand on her shoulder was helping to hold her up.

"Feeling a little dizzy? It should pass in a minute. Using the magic can take a lot out of you. You must always be careful how long you try to keep the magic going. If you do it for too long, you can black out."

Susan and her grandfather examined the hole in the floor where the stone had been. A fine layer of gray dust covered the bottom of the hole, but nothing else seemed to have happened.

Had they failed? After all that they had done, the dragon was still imprisoned in the stones of the cave. Susan was so disappointed that she began to cry.

"Why do you weep, child?" the dragon asked.

"Oh, Prax, I'm so sorry. It didn't work. You're still trapped."

The dragon's laughter echoed like a thunderclap in the small cave.

"Dry your eyes and look more closely, Susan."

Susan looked carefully at the hole where the stone had been. Tiny hairline cracks had appeared in the rocks surrounding the hole.

"But....they're only small cracks."

"The spells that created this prison were woven around me like a garment. Pull on the right thread, and the whole fabric begins to unravel. I can already feel the stones beginning to shift. You should run."

They could feel the floor of the cave starting to rumble under their feet as Cooper grabbed Susan's hand

and started down the tunnel toward the mouth of the cave.

Cooper called out as they ran. "Bodkin! The cave is collapsing. We need to get as far away as possible."

They met Bodkin at the entrance of the cave and ran toward the forest as the ground beneath them shook with increasing intensity.

Once they reached the safety of the trees, all three turned back to watch. The entire hill was moving. Rocks and loose earth were sliding down the sides of the small hill that made up the dragon's prison.

Suddenly the ridge on the top of the hill burst open, sending stones and dirt for a hundred yards in all directions. A huge set of wings emerged from the crater. A tongue of fire shot a thousand feet into the air. Then the dragon's voice boomed out one word that shook the trees surrounding them: "FREE!"

Prax leaped into the air and flew straight up for five hundred feet before turning and diving toward the ground at breakneck speed.

Susan grabbed her grandfather's hand. Had all those years of imprisonment driven Prax mad? She was sure that the dragon was going to crash headfirst into the ground. But in the last ten feet, he pulled up in a sweeping arc, his tail just brushing the grass as the force of the breeze from his wings almost knocked them over. His laughter echoed off the trees as he slowed to make a lazy circle around the clearing.

He was magnificent to watch.

The dragon made one more loop and then landed near the edge of the trees. Susan couldn't help wondering how anything so huge could be so graceful. The dragon was as big as her grandfather's entire workshop.

"My friends, I had almost forgotten how wonderful it is to fly. I don't have enough words to express my thanks, but I must ask you to indulge me for an hour. I have not eaten in over forty years, and my hunger is enormous. There is a herd of deer just over the ridge and a clear lake where I may drink. I shall return within the hour and answer any questions that I am able to."

Prax turned and headed off along the base of the mountain, climbing high into the air as he went. Cooper went to his pack and removed a length of rope. He sat on a stump and started to weave the rope into a pattern.

"Come and sit down, girls. Prax will be back soon. Let me tell you my idea." As promised, the dragon returned in just under an hour. His scales glistened in the sunlight.

"Thank you for your patience, my friends. I was able to catch two plump deer near the lake over the ridge. I could have eaten a dozen, but then I would have needed a nap and I've done quite enough sleeping lately. I went for a short swim to wash away all the dirt and rocks lodged in my scales and was able to catch a fat old catfish for dessert. Now, how can I thank you for my freedom?"

"I have an idea," Cooper said.

Prax laughed out loud as Cooper explained his plan.

"We must certainly do as you suggest, Cooper. I have gained my freedom, had a good meal, and now, a little fun besides. This is turning out to be a fine day."

Cooper placed his hand on the dragon's head and they both closed their eyes. The carvings on Cooper's staff began to glow until both he and the dragon were bathed in blue light. Then as quickly as it had begun, the light faded and went out.

Prax grinned at the three travelers. "As soon as you are ready, we can go."

In the time that Prax was away, Cooper, with the help of the two girls, had woven a large net out of the length of rope from his pack. They tied the net around the neck of the dragon. Cooper placed their gear into the net and then climbed in and tested it to make sure that it was secure. Once he was satisfied that it was safe, he had the two girls climb aboard.

"Hang on, girls. Prax, take us to Kestriana, the palace of the elves!"

Prax took off along the edge of the forest and began a steady climb until they were well above the treetops. He headed northeast away from the mountain. It was breathtaking to see the countryside laid out before them for miles. As they passed over the crystal clear lake where Prax had bathed, they were able to see their own reflection mirrored in the still water. In the distance, near the horizon, they could see the city of the elves.

The wind in their ears made conversation almost impossible, but the scenery was so beautiful that they just sat back in the cargo net and enjoyed the ride.

It wasn't long before Prax banked gently to the right and said, "We approach the city of the elves."

Chapter 4

Lady Coramina was struggling to keep from dozing off. One of the more tedious of her duties as Princess Ashley's scribe was to periodically update the chronicles of the royal family. She had read through some of the old histories so many times that she could recite them from memory. More than once, she had woken up at her desk with her neck aching and her head resting on top of one of the old volumes.

A short walk in the courtyard would be refreshing, but she knew that if she allowed herself to take a break, the chronicles would never get updated and they would still be waiting for her when she came back.

Suddenly, she was jolted wide awake. Her ears rang as if someone had just shouted in them, but there wasn't anyone else in the room.

Coramina had just received a psychic message that was so strong her head was still buzzing. She was out of her chair in an instant, and her hands shook as she yanked open the library door. The chronicles and all of her usual ladylike manners were forgotten as she ran, barefoot, down the corridor shouting for the princess.

Marinus Samarian, king of the elves, was not happy as he looked down at both Lady Coramina, the court psychic, and his daughter, Princess Ashley. . Princess Ashley usually handled most affairs of state without having to disturb him. He didn't like the fact that they had insisted on speaking to him, and he made sure that the two women knew it.

"Well...what is it that is so important that you feel you must barge in here and disturb me?"

"Father, Cora...I mean, the Lady Coramina, has received a message," Ashley answered.

The king was becoming impatient. "Yes, yes, so you have said."

Coramina stepped forward. "The message was sent specifically for you, My Lord. It said, 'The barrel maker, Cooper, requests an audience with King Marinus of the Elves. We will be arriving in the south courtyard within the hour.'"

The king sat upright in his chair. "What? Cooper, the barrel maker? In my courtyard? He is not only a thief, but a liar too. The guards would not even allow him onto the palace grounds. He could never gain access to my private courtyard."

Coramina spoke up again. "I also sensed a second presence, My Lord. A very strong presence. I believe that it was the dragon, Prax."

The king scoffed at her. "Have you been drinking, woman? The dragon? Impossible! Prax vanished decades ago. And why is this man, Cooper, even in my kingdom looking for the dragon? You're responsible for this, aren't you, Ashley?"

"Yes, Father, I'm sorry," Ashley answered, looking at the floor like a scolded child. "Please forgive me for not asking your permission. But if he has actually found Prax, we must hear what he has to say. Cooper can be very resourceful. And I have recently discovered that he has both an amberstone and the use of red magic."

The king scowled. "He has an intact amberstone? And you neglected to tell me this? I told you that he was a thief. You tread on dangerous ground where this man is concerned, Ashley. Besides, he's a human, it's impossible for him to use red magic."

"But not for his granddaughter," the princess responded.

The king settled back into his chair, grumbling. The princess was right, and he knew it. Any news of the dragon could not be ignored, and Cooper would never be so bold as to demand an audience unless his news was important. None of those things made King Marinus feel any happier about being disturbed. "Very well, then...it is a warm day and it is pleasant in the courtyard. You both know how I feel about this man, Cooper, but it may be amusing to watch him make a fool of himself trying to get into my courtyard. I assure you, though, that if this is some sort of a trick, I will banish him for the rest of his life."

Under her breath, Ashley whispered. "You tried that once before."

Prax went into a slow descent until he was only twenty feet above the rooftops. As they flew over the outlying houses and farms, he breathed out a couple of fireballs and sent them high into the air where they dispersed harmlessly. He deliberately circled the city slowly to make certain that all the elves were able to see that he was alive and well.

Finally, he turned toward the castle. He passed over so low that his enormous shadow blanketed the entire courtyard, including the king and princess who waited there. Prax circled one last time before landing so gently that he barely disturbed the grass.

As soon as Cooper and the two girls dismounted and removed their transport net, the dragon swung around to where Princess Ashley and Coramina stood and laid his head on the ground right in front of them, just like Cooper's dog, Cookie, when she wanted to have her ears scratched. The princess immediately started to rub the small soft ridges on the dragon's neck. Cora deftly stepped around the dragon's snout and rubbed the other side. Prax made a sound that reminded them of a cat purring.

"Oh, thank you, ladies. I have so missed these small pleasures," the dragon said. "I cannot properly express my gratitude for my freedom. You heard my cries, and you sent help."

The princess hugged the dragon around the neck. "Dear Prax, You've been gone so long that we almost gave up hope of ever knowing what happened to you."

From across the courtyard, the king was becoming increasingly more annoyed at being ignored.

"When you two ladies are finally done petting the dog, I would like to speak to him," the king snapped at them. Then he spoke directly to the dragon. "So, Prax, tell me where you have been for all these years."

Prax lifted his head, turned to look directly at the King, and quietly answered. "No."

The king rose to his feet. "What!"

Prax looked away as if the king was of no importance. "I will tell my story to the princess and my other friends here. You may listen, if you so wish, *and* if you remain silent."

The face of the king was bright red with anger. He rose from his chair and marched across the courtyard to stand directly in front of the dragon's snout. "How dare you. I am Marinus Samarian, King of the Elves!"

Prax's eyes narrowed to slits and the sides of his mouth drew back to reveal six-inch long teeth as he stared down the king. "No, you *used* to be King of the Elves. Now, you're nothing but a grouchy old recluse. I may have been trapped for forty years, but I am still a dragon. I still possess the ability to watch over your world while I sleep. Princess Ashley rules in your stead while you sit and brood, alone and lonely. You call this man, Cooper, a thief and you direct your anger at him because he married your daughter and took her away from here after *you* drove her from this house. Meanwhile, your stubbornness has caused you to miss out on the lives of your daughter, granddaughter, and now, your great-granddaughter. The king that I once knew was strong and brave. He enjoyed a good wine, a fine meal, and a good laugh with friends. He led his people into battle against an army of gremlins, and I was proud to fight next to him. Where is *that* king? Does he still live, old man!?"

Prax emphasized his last few words with a small puff of smoke from his nostrils.

The courtyard was dead silent as the king and the dragon faced each other.

The king glared silently at the dragon for a moment, then his expression softened and a sad look came into his eyes. He turned and slowly returned to his chair. The princess started toward him, but he waved her off. Even the dragon looked bewildered.

"Oh Prax, old friend. No one has spoken to me in that way for years. Princess Ashley's mother used to talk to me just like that whenever I started getting too full of myself. It was exactly what I needed to awaken me from this cloud of gloom that I have been under since my queen died. Everything that you have said is true. I have wasted years being angry. Please forgive a foolish old elf."

A slight smile crossed the king's face.

"Allow me to have food and drink brought here, then we can all sit and listen. I confess that I have long wondered what ever became of the mighty dragon, Prax. I am eager to hear your story, and I promise to remain silent while you tell it."

"Ho, now there is a glimpse of the king that I once knew. I will gladly wait while a picnic is brought for my friends." The dragon swung his massive head around to address the sentries at the edge of the courtyard. "Guards, bring food and drink for the king and his guests! Quickly, now!"

The guards looked at each other, unsure of what to do.

The king spoke to them. "You heard the dragon. Hurry up. It would be rude to keep my guests waiting. Go and find my squire. He will arrange everything. You do not need to protect me. No one would be fool enough to attack me with a dragon in my courtyard."

The two guards disappeared into the castle, and a few moments later the king's valet rushed into the courtyard followed by servants bringing tables for food.

The valet stared at Prax with a look of sheer terror.

"Sire...do you want us to provide food for the dragon?" he stammered.

Prax answered the trembling man in a booming voice, which caused him to jump about a foot. "No, thank you, Squire, I have eaten just an hour ago, but it is very kind of you to think of me. Well, its old Macilon, isn't it? Didn't I nearly eat you once when you were a young man? Yes, I remember now. Your friends dared you to sneak up behind me and touch my tail while I slept, but I wasn't really asleep. I almost had you for lunch, but you were far too skinny and boney."

"We were boys. It was just a foolish prank. We meant no harm," answered the shaking man.

"I believe I singed the backside of your britches and sent you on your way with a warning to never bother a sleeping dragon again. I do hope you still remember," Prax said with a devious grin.

"Oh yes, My Lord Prax. I have not forgotten. I will never forget." The old squire was quaking as he spoke.

The king chuckled at the obvious embarrassment that Prax's story had caused his stuffy squire. "Macilon, have the servants spread blankets on the grass," the king told him. "We can have a proper picnic."

"Is that wise, Sire? With your arthritis?" the old valet asked.

"You worry too much, Macilon. I have plenty of friends and family to help me get back up if need be. I'll be fine," the king reassured him.

"I'm not certain that your physician would agree, Sire, but we shall do as you ask." The old servant turned to go, clearly anxious to get far away from the dragon as quickly as possible.

"Oh, and Macilon, relax. As the dragon just said, he is not going to eat you or anyone else."

"Yes, Sire. I've spoken to the kitchen staff and they are preparing lunch as we speak, but it will take a few moments."

"Thank you, Macilon. Let us know when they are ready. We will amuse ourselves until then."

Susan tugged on her grandfather's arm and asked, "Grandfather, who is the woman with the princess?"

He leaned down and answered her quietly. "That's Lady Coramina. She's the princess's scribe and assistant. She's also a psychic. She's the one that Prax and I sent the message to."

"She looks just like Mina," Susan commented.

Grandfather smiled. "That's because she's her twin sister."

"Mina's an elf?!" Susan shouted it so loud that everyone in the courtyard stopped and looked.

"Yes, Mina's an elf. She was your grandmother's best friend when they were young, and she came to take care of her when she got sick." Cooper sighed, "That's another one of the things that we've been meaning to tell you. Would you like to meet Mina's sister?"

"Yes, please!" Princess Ashley and Coramina were already on their way across the courtyard after Susan's outburst.

Ashley spoke first. "Hello, Susan. May I introduce the Lady Coramina."

"I'm so pleased to finally meet you, Susan," Coramina said as she extended a delicate hand. "Obviously, your grandfather just told you that your Mina is my sister. The princess and I feel like we already know you. Mina writes to me every week and tells me all about you. She couldn't be prouder of you if you were her own granddaughter."

"It's very nice to meet you. How are you able to get mail here?" Susan asked, puzzled.

When Coramina laughed, Susan noticed that she had the exact same laugh as Mina. "Wysp, carries letters back and forth for us. Did you know that Mina's full name is Saramina? "

"No, I didn't know that. Any time that I've asked her about herself, she has always avoided talking about her family," Susan said. "She always just says that Grandfather and I are her family. When I get home, I'm going to insist that she tell me everything there is to know about you and growing up in this world." Susan turned to the princess. "And Prax told me that you're my aunt."

Ashley bent and gave Susan a hug. "Yes, I wanted so much to tell you earlier but I promised your grandfather that I wouldn't. Your grandmother was my sister, Anna. You remind me so much of her. She would be so proud of you for finding and rescuing Prax."

Susan looked closely at Ashley's face. "There is something that I've been wondering about, if you don't mind my asking. Prax said that you were the older sister, but you look much younger than my grandmother."

Ashley's face lit up in a big smile. "Well, that's the nicest thing that anyone has said to me in a long time. Prax was right. I was older than Anna, but we age more slowly here. My father, the king, is over a hundred years old."

Coramina took Susan's hand and said, "Come, sit with me and tell me about my sister. She always talks about you and your grandfather in her letters, but never says much about herself."

The dragon, the king, and even lunch, were temporarily forgotten as Susan and Coramina immediately got into a lively conversation about Mina.

Small groups started to break off while they waited for the staff to set up the lunch. Cooper headed for the far side of the courtyard to chat with Korin, the princess's bodyguard.

Princess Ashley pulled aside one of the servants and whispered in his ear. He disappeared into the castle and returned a few moments later carrying a finely crafted bow that Ashley had asked the man to retrieve from her quarters. She quietly crossed the courtyard to where Bodkin stood.

"Bodkin, I did not have the chance to thank you earlier for your actions to protect me from the attack by the falcon. You exhibited considerable prowess with the bow," Ashley said.

"Thank you, My Lady. That is high praise coming from you. Your skills with the bow are well known," Bodkin responded.

"I've had one of the servants bring my bow down from my quarters. Would you like to see it?" Ashley asked.

"Yes, very much, Princess." Bodkin could barely contain her excitement. It was common knowledge that the Princess was an excellent shot and that she possessed one of the finest bows in the land. Bodkin carefully accepted the bow from the servant. The craftsmanship was exquisite. It was carved of a rich, dark wood that glistened in the sunlight. The grip was adorned with inlays of dragon's tooth ivory. It was so finely balanced that it felt like an extension of Bodkin's arm, and when she tried the pull, the action was smooth and fluid. Though it was a little stiff for her, she had no doubt that it would be perfect for a grown woman like the princess.

Bodkin was beaming as she gently handed it back to the servant. "It is a beautiful weapon, Princess. Thank you for showing it to me."

Ashley answered with a sly smile. "A little friendly contest while we wait?"

After a few seconds of surprise, Bodkin's face broke into a big smile.

"Certainly, My Lady. I will gladly accept your challenge. But be warned that even though you are the princess, I will shoot to win and show you no special treatment. What shall we be shooting at?"

"There are dozens of apples on the ground under the old tree at the edge of the courtyard." Ashley turned toward the dragon. "Prax, are you still able to flick green apples into the air with your tail, or have you gotten too old?"

Prax raised his head up. "Princess, you wound me with such questions. I most certainly can still toss apples into the air. Are you still skilled enough to shoot at them without puncturing my tail?"

Ashley laughed at him. "Well, that tail is a pretty big target. But I believe that I can manage to avoid hitting it."

"Then I will be happy to participate in your contest," Prax answered, grinning. "And Marinus will keep score. Who would make a better judge than the king himself?"

Everyone held their breath as they waited for the king's answer.

"That sounds like it would be fun. We haven't had a good competition for quite some time. But I will warn you, young Bodkin, the princess is very good with that bow. She has never been beaten...at least not yet. Let the contest begin, and may the best woman win," the king announced with a wave of his hand.

Prax scooped up a pair of apples with his broad tail. "If you two ladies are ready," he said as he sent the two apples high into the air with a flip of his tail.

Both girls fired and both arrows skewered their respective apples. The next three throws went exactly the same, with both archers cleanly hitting their targets. After the first few simple throws, Prax began to make it more challenging, throwing apples far and wide. He even managed to put some backspin on some that caused them to wobble erratically. Every time, both participants hit their targets.

The score was dead even on accuracy, but the king gave the younger Bodkin the advantage on speed as she always managed to get her shot off a split second faster.

"Better be careful, Daughter, or this young girl may best you," the king called out to Ashley.

Determination showed on the princess's face as she waited for Prax's next throw. In one last spectacular shot, the princess paused just a second for Bodkin to shoot, then she turned and split both Bodkin's apple and the arrow that pierced it with her shot.

The courtyard was silent as the entire crowd was awestruck by the princess's amazing shot. Then the silence erupted into cheers as the king declared Princess Ashley the winner. Once Bodkin got over her amazement at the princess's skill, she graciously conceded that it was an incredible shot.

Just then, Macilon announced that lunch was ready. The kitchen staff had laid out a fine lunch. There was dark bread that was sweet and warm and smelled like it had just come out of the oven, and a thick stew made with hearty vegetables. Next to that was cold venison and pork, sliced thin as paper, and a tangy cheese that had a wonderful aroma. At the other end of the table was a wide variety of fruits in all different shapes and colors.

Bodkin slipped in next to Susan and whispered in her ear, "Try the dark red berries, but only one at a time. They're so sweet that they'll make you dizzy if you eat more than one at a time."

Susan popped one of the berries into her mouth and was certain that she had never tasted anything so sweet before. As she continued down the length of the table, Susan sampled many of the fruits and breads. Everything tasted wonderful.

Two members of the kitchen staff were passing out mugs filled with a drink that Susan thought tasted a lot like lemonade, but just a little different.

The staff helped fill plates and made sure that everyone was seated on the blankets with plenty to eat before disappearing back into the castle.

When everyone was comfortably seated, Prax began his tale.

"My story begins before the war with the gremlins started. Some of you here were present at that time and know parts of my story already, so I will direct my tale to my two young rescuers, Susan and Bodkin.

"Long before the first attack, my brethren and I became aware of the fact that the gremlins were amassing an army against the elves. The elves had long been friends and allies of the dragons, so we were concerned for their safety. No sensible creature ever craves war. The gremlins, on the other hand, had never been very friendly towards the dragons, but they had rather painfully learned long ago that it was best to leave us in peace and we had no quarrel with them. The elves already knew what the gremlins were planning, and the elf army was well trained and organized. There was no need for me or any of my kind to become involved, so we just observed from a distance, as is our usual custom.

"Early on in the conflict, the gremlins were fierce and bloodthirsty fighters, but they were little more than rabble. They had little or no training and poor leadership. The elves were beating them back on every flank. Then something changed.

"The gremlins attacks became more planned and precise. It quickly became clear that someone new had started to lead them, but no one knew who their new leader was.

"Then, while the elves were scrambling to revise their battle strategy, the Hall of Conjurers was attacked and totally decimated. All of the amberstones at the hall were destroyed, shattered into tiny pieces. One of the few survivors told of how the attack had been led by the creature known as the lindworm with the gremlins following behind and savagely hunting down and butchering anyone who survived the initial assault.

"We still didn't know who was directing the gremlins, but the attack did tell us a few things. Apparently, the person leading the gremlins was a powerful magic-wielder who was ruthless enough to eliminate any resistance from the Guild of Magic. They would need considerable skill just to locate the lindworm and then some strong magic to protect themselves long enough to reason with the monster and convince him to help them in their battle against the elves. The lindworm had no loyalty to the gremlins; he would have devoured them as easily as he would the elves. But the war fed his appetite for chaos and death. He was only interested in destruction."

Susan spoke up. "Excuse me for interrupting, Prax, but what is a lindworm? I've never heard of one before."

Prax answered with a tooth-filled grin. "An excellent question, Susan. And an important part of my story. Very few know the history of the beast. I doubt that even our court scribe, Lady Coramina, knows where the beast came from."

"I've only seen it mentioned twice in the chronicles that are dated before the war. They only say that the lindworm was a creature that left devastation wherever it appeared. During the war, the chronicles state little more than what you have just told us— that the monster existed, it destroyed the Hall of Conjurors, and it was helping the gremlins. They never mention anything about its origins," Coramina answered.

"That is not surprising. I am probably the only living creature left who knows how the lindworm came to be. The lindworm was an abomination, a freak offshoot of the dragon bloodline. You could say that he was a distant relative of mine.

"Centuries ago, a very foolish wizard stole a dragon's egg. He believed that if he placed a spell on the egg, that when it hatched, the young dragon would obey him and become his servant. He was not a very good wizard, and the spell went horribly wrong.

"Magic is part of a dragon's essence, and we are affected by it differently than other creatures. It is never wise to tamper with such things. The egg hatched into a freak half-dragon with no wings and only two legs. The young hatchling was insane, wanting only destruction and chaos. The female dragon whose egg had been stolen eventually tracked down the foolish wizard, ate him, and would have killed the young hatchling, but the half-dragon was already gone. Some believe that he escaped through the Ice Caves into the Scandinavian countries of the human world. Over the years, he remained hidden in the darkness, deep underground. The local folk believed that he was a giant snake or worm, which is where he acquired the name lindworm. They sometimes offered him sacrifices of gold or young maidens.

"The half-dragon understood that if the other dragons found him, they would destroy him in the same way that people in your world would put down a rabid dog. As he grew to full size, alone in the dark, his madness also grew. When he finally returned to the surface in this world, he mated with a young female dragon, producing freakish creatures that spread disease and created havoc. Eventually, my kin had no choice but to hunt them down and destroy them. But they were elusive and hard to find. As soon as we learned that the creature and what still remained of his brood were helping the gremlins, we joined the elf cause.

"As soon as the lindworm realized that we were pursuing him, he abandoned his offspring and went back into hiding. Although he was still the largest and the strongest of the freaks, he knew that he could not survive a direct confrontation with a clutch of dragons.

"Unknown to us, he had inherited a quality from our distant relatives, the vipers. The lindworm possessed fangs and venom that was powerful enough to kill even dragons. Although he was insane, he could be very cunning. He set out to destroy his pursuers. He ambushed and killed many of the dragons that hunted him, often using his malformed children as bait, sending them out to be slaughtered like sheep. Many of my kind died from his poisonous bite, including my mate. With the death of each dragon and the elf army being forced backwards by the monstrous creatures, the gremlin army grew stronger and bolder, advancing across the countryside toward Kestriana and the city of the elves.

"Finally, all of his offspring were gone and only the lindworm and I remained. He was a dark stain on all of dragon kind, and he needed to be destroyed. I vowed to kill him or die trying. I almost did both.

"I knew that I would have to lure him to the surface. His usual tactic was to burrow just beneath the ground next to one of his freakish children or some other bit of bait that would attract a single dragon out into the open. He would allow the dragon to attack and destroy his offspring, tiring themselves out and often suffering injuries in the process, then he would attack from below, burying his fangs deep into the soft underside of the neck. He would pump as much venom as possible into his victims in a few seconds, then release them and escape back underground before they had a chance to counter-attack.

"My plan was extremely risky. I would have to use myself as bait to lure him out. I would only have a second to react when he attacked. If I failed, I would die. Even if I was successful, I might still die from his bite.

"When the gremlin army began its assault, he was lying in wait near the front line. He expected me to meet the attack head-on, in the usual fashion. Instead, I flew high above the field of battle and dove toward them with the sun directly behind me. When I was only ten feet above them, I pulled up, flew right over the top of the entire Gremlin Army, reversed direction, and attacked them from the rear. I was too far away for the lindworm to ambush, and the only escape route for the gremlins was directly into the path of the elven archers.

"After many years of living underground, the lindworm's hearing was finely tuned to footsteps from above. He could tell where a creature was and which direction it was moving just by listening. The panic in the ranks of the gremlins confused his delicate hearing.

"As I began my attack, I moved erratically from side to side, stomping my feet and thumping my tail against the ground. I even leapt into the air and flew fifty feet in one direction or another in a further effort to confuse him.

"When he finally broke through the surface and tried to attack, I was thirty feet to the side and out of his reach.

"He was forced to stand and fight. If he tried to turn and retreat underground, I would be on him before he could burrow away and he was done for.

"Even without his poisonous bite, he was a formidable enemy. He was as big and powerful as any dragon, and he could whip his tail around with lightning speed and the force of a battering ram.

"He shrieked out his anger at me as we faced each other, slowly circling as each of us feinted and probed each other's defenses trying to find an opening. I managed to strike a solid blow to the side of his head with my wing and was almost on top of him, but he was as fast as a cobra and dodged my attack, smashing his tail into my wing and injuring it.

"In strength and size, we were evenly matched and neither of us could gain an advantage. I knew that I would have to try a desperate gamble. I allowed myself to stumble and turn to the side, and he instantly struck me in the hind leg with a devastating blow from his tail. I immediately started to back away, dragging my back leg and allowing him to believe that I was badly injured, knowing that the monster would try to come in for the kill.

"As he lunged for my throat, I leapt up and spun in midair. His fangs bit down on the iron hard scales of my tail instead of the soft flesh of my throat. One fang snapped off immediately, but the second one managed to slide between two scales and just pierce the skin beneath, injecting a small amount of venom before it also broke off. I came down hard and drove my full weight onto his back, snapping his spine and pinning him to the ground as he snarled and twisted. With my claws deeply embedded in his back, I bit down on the back of his neck, and with every ounce of strength that I had left, I twisted and pulled. The monster's neck made a terrible sound as it tore in half and, with one last twist, I pitched his severed head into the middle of the gremlin forces.

"The sight of the lindworm's bloody head in their midst, with the jaws still snapping open and closed, panicked what remained of the Gremlin Army and destroyed their will to fight. They broke ranks and ran from the battlefield like frightened rabbits. Within two minutes of the destruction of the lindworm, the battle was over.

"But I had no time to savor the victory. My rear leg was broken, my wing was injured, and I had been poisoned with the creature's venom. I knew that I could not survive long. Even a small amount of the monster's poison in my veins could kill. It would just take longer. I had one chance. I had to get as far away as possible and place myself into a state of dragon sleep."

Coramina spoke up. "Dragon sleep? I've read all the books of dragon lore in the castle library, but I've never heard of dragon sleep."

"That is by design, My Lady. Except for a very few select members of the Guild of Magic, all of whom are either dead or lost, no human or elf has ever been told of the dragon sleep until now.

"Many have wondered why some of my brethren disappear for long periods of time, sometimes years. The dragon sleep is the reason. We have the ability to place ourselves in a sleep-like state. Creatures in Susan's world do a similar thing that they call hibernation, only with dragons everything slows to a near death-like state. We can draw the magic from the earth itself, and all of that energy is then channeled into our ability to heal ourselves. If a dragon is injured or ill, the sleep can halt any further damage or injury and begin to restore them. But it is a very slow process, and the more severe the injury, the longer it will take to recover. We are totally helpless at that time. That is the reason that no dragon has ever revealed this secret before. We could easily be slaughtered like sheep while we sleep.

"To conceal and protect ourselves, we will usually bury ourselves near the base of a mountain, leaving only a tiny corridor for fresh air. Anyone coming upon our hiding place would dismiss it as a minor rock slide. The air hole just appears to be a small rabbit hole, and even if it should become blocked, we would not suffocate. This is why I fled after the battle. It was imperative that I began the process before the venom could spread too far into my veins. I have been at the base of Mistral Mountain, buried under a mound of earth, slowly purging myself of the poison and healing my wounds, for the last forty years.

"My body recovered twenty years ago, but as I started to awaken, I discovered that I was unable to move, imprisoned in a web of magic. Someone from the Guild of Magic had betrayed our secret. I have little doubt that my prison was created by the same person who led the gremlins, destroyed the Guild of Magic and, if this person is still alive, is secretly watching from somewhere nearby while plotting some new evil.

"I would probably still be trapped there, but fortunately my kind has the ability to navigate the dream world. Usually we can only observe the dreams of others, but there are rare occasions when we can break through into those dreams. I have spent the last twenty years searching for special individuals whose dreams I could enter. Years ago, I found someone, another magic-wielder. I believe that she was a woman, but it is impossible to tell in the dream world, and she would not identify herself. I am certain that she was not the one who imprisoned me. When I asked for her aid she said that she could not help me without exposing her existence which would place her in grave danger and she, very likely, would not live long enough to help me if that happened. She did allow me to come and speak to her from time to time which I believe helped to keep me from going insane.

"After years of searching, I was able to find the Lady Coramina. It took me some time to break through because, being a psychic, if she were to leave her mind open and unprotected, both good and bad spirits could enter her dreams. I tried many times until, finally, she was able to hear me. Even then, I could only communicate with images of my plight and where I was. Fortunately, I chose well and she was able to piece together my messages and, with the help of the princess, send my brave new friends to free me.

"That is how I came to be here with all of you today. I do not have enough words to express my gratitude to all who helped me regain my freedom. Thank you, my friends."

The courtyard was silent for a moment after Prax finished his story; finally, King Marinus spoke. "An incredible story, Prax. Lady Coramina, you will see to it that Prax's story will be recorded in the chronicles?"

"Every word, My Lord," Coramina answered. "I have already sent one of the servants to the library to retrieve pen and paper so I can record his story while all the details are fresh in my mind. Do you wish me to record the secret of the dragon sleep, or should that remain hidden?"

"I believe that I may be the only one of my kind left," Prax answered, "so recording my secret should not endanger anyone but myself. If I discover more of my kin, my first task will be to warn them that someone has revealed the secret of the dragon sleep and tried to destroy me using that knowledge. Our secret is a secret no longer, so you may write down all that I have told you."

"Excellent. Lady Coramina, please record every word for the archives," King Marinus said. "Then, as King of the Elves, I have just one more request to ask of you, Prax. Stay and spend a few hours relaxing with me, two old war horses sharing stories. It is a fine day, and we have some catching up to do."

Prax gave the king a tooth-filled grin. "That is a command that I will gladly obey. Have old Macilon bring your chair over next to me so we can talk."

Cooper stood up. "I'll bring it. I'm not sure Macilon's old heart can take the strain of being that close to you."

The dragon chuckled. "You spoil my fun, barrel maker, but, you are probably right."

The king and the dragon spent the rest of the day and well into the evening discussing old friends and reliving treasured adventures.

Chapter 5

The sunlight was streaming into the window as Susan opened her eyes. Bodkin was already up, dressed, and across the room that they shared, sampling from the breakfast tray of fruits and pastries that had been provided by the kitchen.

"It's about time you woke up," Bodkin said. "Better get moving. If you don't hurry, Prax will be gone before you get there."

Susan rolled quickly out of bed and started to dress. Prax had become one of her newest friends and she had made a special promise to him to come and see him off in the morning. She was not about to be the only one to miss out on saying goodbye to him. She jammed a Danish in her mouth as she pulled on her hiking boots and headed out the door.

"Some friend you are," she mumbled to Bodkin through a mouthful of pastry. "Why didn't you wake me?"

"Relax, if you hadn't gotten up in the next five minutes, I would have shaken you. I knew that it would only take you a minute to get dressed, and we can get down to the courtyard in two minutes. We won't be late," Bodkin replied.

She was right, as a moment later, the two girls were racing each other down the steps and heading for the courtyard. Most of the adults were already there. There was no need to ask if Prax had left yet; he was visible from half the windows in the castle. When he spread his wings, his huge frame took up one entire corner of the courtyard.

Cooper was chatting with Princess Ashley as they approached.

"Good morning, Grandfather. Good morning, Aunt Ashley," Susan said.

The princess answered with a gentle smile. "Aunt Ashley. Oh, I like the sound of that. Good morning, Susan. And to you, Bodkin."

"Morning, Princess," the elf girl responded with a huge smile. Bodkin was still in awe of everything around her. A few days ago, she would never have dreamed that one day she would be an honored guest in the castle and on a first name basis with the princess.

There was no time for small talk as the door on the opposite side of the courtyard opened and the king arrived. He was alone except for his old valet, Macilon, and even though the king and the dragon had talked late into the night, trading old stories of friends that were long gone, he strode across the grass with a friendly smile and a spring in his step that had been absent for the last twenty years. He crossed to his usual seat where a number of additional chairs had been set up.

"Susan, please come and sit next to me," the King said. "Bodkin, if you would sit on the other side. And bring my daughter with you. I would like to have my family close to me."

The two girls quickly came and sat on either side of the king while Princess Ashley stepped behind the king's chair and stood with her hand resting gently on his shoulder.

When Prax saw that everyone was assembled, he addressed the small group.

"My dear friends. Thank you so much for coming to see me off. Words fail me. I cannot express my gratitude to you all. You have become my new family, and it saddens me to have to leave."

Princess Ashley approached from where she stood and hugged Prax around his massive neck. "Years ago, your bravery ended the war and saved our kingdom. Now that you are free, where will you go?" the princess asked.

The dragon's eyes took on a faraway look. "While I was imprisoned, my only contact with the outside world was through the world of dreams. More than once, I thought that I heard the distant whispers of dragon voices in the dreamscape, but when I called out to them, they faded away and vanished. I have long wondered if I truly was the last of my kind; but if I have survived, others may have also. When I leave here, I will go in search of any of my brethren who may still live. I will not rest until I know for certain if any of them still exist. If I am fortunate enough to find any of my kind, I will try to persuade them to join me and, together, we will go in search of the renegade magic-wielder that imprisoned me. I have a score to settle, and he still poses a great danger to this world. Perhaps during our search we will also discover the second magic-wielder, the one who was kind to me in the dream world. I would like to find her and thank her for her kindness. Sadly, we do not know who she may be or where her loyalties lie. She may not be a friend of the elves. I would caution you to be wary, Marinus of the Elves. You have hidden enemies beyond these walls."

The king rose and approached Prax. "Your warning is well taken, old friend. We wish you god speed in your quest, and know that you will always be welcome in the kingdom of the elves. But we know of no other dragons having been seen or heard of since the end of the Gremlin Wars. Where will you begin your search?"

"I will return to my birthplace, high in the Yurt Mountains. Deep inside, all dragons are still wild creatures. We are born and bred on the mountain ridges. That is where we first learn to soar on the thermals and see the world from high above. It is where young dragons can try out their fire, melting a hole in the side of a glacier. Where they learn that only a roar of the proper pitch and volume can start an avalanche on a high pass. It is my home. If any of my kind still live and they are able, that is where they will return to. Even if they are hidden there, I will be able to find them. That is where I will go to begin my search.

"There is one more thing before I go. If I can have a private word with my two young rescuers, Susan and Bodkin." Both girls approached and leaned in close as Prax spoke to them very softly. "I have a special gift for the two of you. There is a secret way for you to contact me that no one else knows of. If you whisper my name three times, just before you go to sleep, it will linger with your thoughts and call out to me from the dreamscape. Then my dream self will be able to find you and look in on your dreams. I can chase away the nightmares and you can talk to me. If something special should happen to one of us, we can tell each other in our dreams and we'll remember it when we awaken. If your need is dire, call me and I will come."

The two girls both hugged the dragon's neck and then returned to stand next to the king as Prax raised his head and stretched out his wings. "Marinus, I shall return within a year. We still have many stories to share. Please do not be foolish enough to die before then."

The king laughed as he answered, "I shall try very hard to honor that request."

Prax gave the king a tooth-filled grin. "Now it is time for me to go. Farewell, my friends."

Everyone gathered in the courtyard took a few steps back as the dragon leapt high into the air and with a few powerful beats of leathery wings was quickly over the courtyard wall and headed away towards the distant mountains. The small group in the courtyard waved and watched until Prax was little more than a dot on the distant skyline.

After Prax's departure, Cooper and the two girls were about to return to their rooms and prepare to resume their journey to the Golden Willow when Korin approached them.

"Would you mind having a few extra traveling companions, my friend?" he asked Cooper. "You and I also have many old stories to trade with each other, and the princess would very much like to spend some time getting to know her new found niece and her friend. Cora would also like to join us. It's been years since we have gone anywhere together. Our separate duties here keep us from spending time with each other as often as we would like, and a short visit to the Golden Willow would be a pleasant vacation from the routine at the castle. Many years have gone by since the last time we were there, and they say that the fairies will dance under the full moon."

Cooper answered with a sigh. "Well....our original plan was just for a quiet weekend so Susan and Bodkin could spend some time together. So far, it hasn't worked out quite as planned. You know that I would greatly enjoy your company, but the two girls have been planning this visit for some time and it would be unfair to deprive them of their time together. I will leave the final decision up to them. Susan, Bodkin, what do you think? Do you mind if Korin, Princess Ashley, and Coramina come along with us?"

The two girls huddled together, giggling, for a moment before Susan answered. "Well, as long as you can keep up and you promise not to wander off. We don't have time to babysit any of you."

"She has inherited some of your wit, Cooper," Korin responded with a hearty laugh. "We'll do our best. We can be ready to leave within the hour. We'll meet you at the north gate."

An hour later, as promised, Korin, Princess Ashley, Lady Coramina and two of the princess's guards were waiting patiently by the north gate when Cooper and the two girls arrived. They were all dressed for hiking and carried lightweight packs.

"Excellent," Cooper said as he and the two girls approached the small group. "Everyone is here. If we maintain a steady pace, we should easily reach the willow by late afternoon."

The group headed away from the castle as a lone snicker, perched atop the gate, stood up, stretched and trotted off to find his mistress.

Everyone was in good spirits after seeing Prax off, and the miles passed quickly. Korin and Coramina had quietly gotten married many years earlier, and their only son had just recently left home. This was their first chance in a very long time to spend some time just for themselves, and they were enjoying every moment together.

By late afternoon, the group arrived at the edge of the glade of the Golden Willow and set up a small camp on the outskirts of the glade. Korin had packed some dried foods provided by the castle's kitchen staff, and he proved to be an excellent camp chef, whipping up a fine stew while Cooper and the princess gathered some local greens to make a tasty salad. After dinner, they all sat together in a circle, chatting and speculating on whether or not the fairies would come and dance.   It was just turning dusk and the evening sky was fading to gray when the first lights began to show themselves. As the travelers watched, they saw what looked like fireflies in the center of the glade. Only a few at first, then more started to appear. They began to come faster and faster, materializing out of thin air, all joining together to form a slowly revolving circle of lights in the air. The entire glade began to take on a soft glow, as if lit by a thousand candles. The circle continued to grow and expand as hundreds of the tiny fairies joined in. Then the music started.

The Golden Willow was singing. It began as little more than a whisper, emanating from every blade of grass and leaf in the glade. It slowly increased to become a beautiful melody. The song of the willow was the most soothing sound any of them had ever heard. They could feel the rhythm of the music flowing from the ground beneath them. The circle of lights slowly grew into a column as the fairies followed each other upward in an ascending spiral to a height of fifty feet. There they dispersed in all directions and slowly spun and twisted and tumbled gracefully as they settled gently back to the grass like snowflakes, only to rejoin the column at the bottom and repeat the cycle. Their dance had created a fountain of living light.

As they danced, the fairies' lights began to change colors. The different types of fairies all seemed to have their own special colors. A group of pixies shone bright crimson on Susan's right, while the sprites that were coming together on the left glowed azure blue. The nymphs overhead twinkled in saffron yellow, and the imps sparkled in emerald green. The colored fairies all joined hands and formed living globes which swirled around the glade in slowly decreasing circles until they veered close enough to be swept up into the column of light. When the balls of colored fairies reached the top of the column, they flew apart like exploding fireworks. It was a dazzling show. The entire group was mesmerized.

A small number of fairies broke off from the main group and surrounded Bodkin. They pushed and prodded her until they coaxed her to her feet and began to draw her into the circle. She looked back at the adults, unsure whether to go. Coramina waved her on. "Go and dance with them, girl. The chronicles say that it's a great honor to be invited to dance with the fairies. They only pick very special people."

That was all the encouragement needed as Bodkin ran into the glade and joined in the fairy dance. As she reached the center of the glade, the fairies instantly began to follow and mirror her movements. When she raised her arms, they flew high into the sky. She brought her arms down and the fairies covered the ground like a blanket of colored moving lights. She twirled and the fairies swirled around her with their brightest colors. She leapt high in the air and the fairies highlighted her every move. The music rose to a crescendo as she danced faster and faster. The fairies laughed and sang with the music as she danced with them, and their voices sounded like the tinkling of a thousand tiny bells. Finally, unable to keep up with the fairies any longer, Bodkin collapsed into a heap in the center of the glade and instantly fell sound asleep as the music slowed to a soft lullaby. A hundred fairies gently lifted her and carried her back to where Korin and Coramina sat. There they carefully laid the sleeping elf girl on a blanket at the couple's feet. Coramina covered Bodkin with a second blanket as she slept, a glowing smile lighting up her face.

As Susan watched, she noticed a dark figure off to the side of the glade. At first she thought that it was one of the princess's guards, but when she looked over, she saw that they both remained at their usual posts, twenty yards behind the princess. If anyone else saw the figure, they did not acknowledge it. Korin and Coramina sat together with the sleeping Bodkin in front of them, and Cooper sat with his back to an old oak tree. Princess Ashley sat next to Cooper with one hand on his arm and her head resting on his shoulder. They were all captivated by the beautiful show of lights and movement provided by the dancing fairies.

The figure motioned to Susan, and she felt compelled to go and speak to it. None of her companions seemed to notice as Susan rose and started toward the side of the glade where the shadowy figure stood. She passed by them as if she was invisible. As she got closer, the person stepped out of the shadow of the trees.

"Hello, Susan," the person said.

"Grandma Anna?" Susan asked. She knew it couldn't be her, but as the figure moved into the soft light of the glade, Susan could see that the strange visitor among the trees looked exactly like her grandmother.

"No, Susan, I only appear to be your grandmother. I am called the Spirit of the Golden Willow. I have no control over who I will look like, and I appear differently to everyone. I just know that I will always take on the form of someone that you love and trust. Don't worry. None of your friends can see me, and if they happen to look over this way, they will believe that you are still sitting there watching the fairies with the rest of them. Please come and walk with me. We're perfectly safe. Nothing can harm us here."

Susan wasn't sure how she knew, but somehow she was certain that the spirit was telling the truth and that she was completely safe. Susan fell into step with the spirit as she slowly walked among the trees that surrounded the glade.

"I remember both your mother and your grandmother coming to watch the fairies dance. And your grandfather's hair has grayed a bit since the last time he was here," the spirit said. "Your grandfather is the reason that I came to speak to you. There are forces at work in the land that are planning a great evil, and it focuses on him. I only see glimpses of these things, and I cannot tell where this evil comes from or what form it will take. But I do know that it will wreak terrible havoc on this land, and the fairies tell me that your grandfather is at the heart of it. They are creatures of magic and can sense these things. They also tell me that you and your friend Bodkin hold the keys to the outcome. The two of you need to help and protect him. Hold out your hands, Susan. I have something to give you that will aid you in your task."

Susan extended her hands, and the spirit placed a small round object in them.

"It's an amberstone!" Susan gasped. It was perfectly round, but smaller than the one that her grandfather had.

"This is my gift to you. The gift of the Golden Willow. I will reveal a secret to you. In your world, amber is created when the resin of the tree, its lifeblood, seeps out and, after many years hardens like stone. Here, in this world, the ground itself contains magic. My roots go deep into the earth and draw the magic out. My resin becomes infused with the magic. It can take as much as a century for me to extract enough magic to form a stone. That is how the amberstones of old came to be centuries ago. This one is small because it has only been fifty years since it began to form, but it still contains great power. Be very careful who you reveal its existence to. When the time comes, use it wisely and do not let it fall into the wrong hands."

"I promise," Susan replied as the spirit produced a small bag on a cord. Susan carefully placed the stone in the bag and hung the cord around her neck, hiding it under her shirt.

The Spirit of the Golden Willow gently took Susan's hand. "Come, it is time that you get back to your friends." As they turned and started back to the glade, Susan began to get very sleepy.

From where Shirell watched, she saw Susan, rise and wander off, following what appeared to be a cloud of smoke. Shirell was certain that the smoke hid an ancient fairy creature, almost certainly a dryad, a tree spirit that was bonded to the Golden Willow. She was not fooled by such a simple deception, but she also knew that it would be incredibly dangerous to approach or interfere. Very few of these creatures still existed, but the ones that did possessed magic of immeasurable power. Shirell was no fool. She would continue to observe the group of travelers as they watched the fairies dance, and she would patiently wait for Susan to return. She felt a touch of sadness knowing that long ago, in what felt like a previous lifetime, she would have enjoyed watching the dancing fairies.

The sun rose on a beautiful morning. A warm breeze blew gently through the glade as the small group of travelers rose, ate a leisurely breakfast, and packed up their gear. No one was in any hurry to leave the calm serenity of the glade.

Susan awoke feeling refreshed but unsure about the events of the night before. It was all so incredible. Did she really speak with the Spirit of the Golden Willow, or was it just a vivid dream? She couldn't remember walking back to the glade or anything else after speaking to the spirit. She quickly reached inside her shirt and found that the small bag containing the stone was safely around her neck. She had not imagined the entire thing. It had been real.

The elves had planned to travel on with Cooper and the girls as far as Pen's camp near the Gnome Door where they would split up. Cooper and Susan would leave Bodkin there with her brother and return home through the gnome door. Ashley and the other elves would continue back to the castle on their own. The weather was nearly perfect, and by mid-morning they were more than half way to their destination.

In the last two days, it had quickly become apparent to Susan that there was a certain attraction between her grandfather and the princess. They walked beside each other all morning, quietly chatting and laughing.

Susan moved up to walk alongside the scribe. "Lady Coramina, may I ask you something?"

Coramina answered with a smile "Certainly, Susan. Ask whatever you like, although I don't think I have to be a psychic to guess what your question is about. But please, call me Cora. There's no need to be so formal once we're away from the castle."

Susan stumbled trying to find the right words. "Well, it's just...is the princess in love with my grandfather?" Susan blurted out.

"That's a difficult question, Susan," Cora said. "I honestly don't know what's in the princess's heart, but if you wish, I can tell you a bit of their history."

"Yes, I would like to know about my grandfather when he was young," Susan responded.

"Well," Coramina began, "I believe that you already know that when your grandfather and his friend first arrived here, they began working for the two elf brothers at the Dragon's Breath pub. Of course, it didn't take long for word of their presence, and of their success at producing a better ale, to get to the castle, and they were called before the king. Even Quisp knew better than to ignore a request from the castle. Their entire workshop was packed up and moved to a location near the castle. They were given apprentices to train and were treated like honored guests. It took a few months, but once the new shop was set up and they had a trained staff, they found that they had a lot of free time on their hands. The two of them quickly became friends with some of the young people at the castle, including the princess, my sister and I, Korin, and a few others that were all of about the same age. They were both eager to learn some of the elven arts and skills including healing, fighting, and even magic. Years earlier, the wizard Eldred had discovered that the ability to do magic is, for lack of a better word, a talent, and everyone has a trace of magic in them. Some people can sing or play music, some are good athletes, some can make beautiful art, and some are quite adept at magic. With training, practice, and a talisman to focus the magic, certain humans are just as skillful as elves. Your grandfather proved to be one of them.

"Weapons training was led by the captain of the guards, and we were treated like any young soldier. Ashley was the fiercest fighter in the group, and she quickly chose Cooper as her sparring partner. As a human, he was bigger and stronger than all the elves, and he was the only one in the group that she couldn't defeat. They usually fought to a draw. And like most young people, it wasn't long before they began a whirlwind romance. They became the talk of the castle. Of course, it was considered scandalous behavior. The princess and a human. The king was furious, and that made it all the more exciting for them.

"Back then, Ashley was brash and impulsive, so when the captain asked her to lead Cooper, his friend John, and a half a dozen other young elves on a scouting mission, she was disappointed. The captain was trying to develop her leadership skills, but she didn't think that a routine scouting mission was exciting enough. She didn't believe that there were any gremlin patrols for miles around, so she didn't bother taking some of the usual precautions. In her haste to get back to the castle, she took a shortcut through a dense stand of trees and into a blind thicket without bothering to scout ahead first.

"It was a beginner's mistake that took a terrible toll. She led them right into an ambush. The instant that they entered the thicket, gremlins appeared from behind every tree and bush. They were surrounded by nearly thirty attackers with no escape route. Ashley and Cooper were in the lead, and instantly a handful of attackers moved to cut them off from the others. They each faced three armed opponents while the remaining ambushers overwhelmed their companions.

"Cooper's broadsword dispatched the first two of his opponents in the initial rush. Ashley was holding off two gremlins with her long knives, but she was unaccustomed to fighting multiple opponents. The times that the captain covered that part of their training, she hadn't paid much attention, arrogantly believing that she was skilled enough to defeat anyone that attacked her. She forgot to protect her flank, and a third attacker rushed her from her blind side. Cooper anticipated the attack, broke off from his last opponent, and was moving to intercept the third gremlin; but before he could cross the distance between them, the creature ducked under the princess's blade and buried his dagger into her side. Ashley screamed and started to go down as Cooper's sword sliced the backstabbing gremlin completely in two before it could move in to finish her.

"Cooper stood over the injured Ashley and fought like a cornered animal. It was as if a blood lust had taken over him, and he slaughtered his attackers until he was ankle deep in blood and no one else remained standing. After the last gremlin fell, he knelt and bound up Ashley's side, picked her up, and carried her back to the camp, running most of the way. He managed to stumble back into the camp, turned her over to the healers, took two steps, and promptly collapsed.

"He was covered in so much gore that the healers were forced to strip him almost naked to find the dozen different wounds that he was bleeding from. He had ignored his own injuries until he knew that Ashley was safe. Both your grandfather and the princess barely made it through that first night. It took three days until Cooper was back on his feet, and it was a full two weeks until Ashley was up and moving around. None of the others returned.

"A patrol was quickly sent back to the site of the ambush. Gremlins sometimes hung captives on stakes and left them to die slowly and painfully of exposure. If any of their companions survived the initial attack, there was still a slight chance that they might be saved. The patrol reported that the carnage was horrifying. The bodies of two of the elves were recovered, but they were unable to find any trace of your grandfather's friend, John.

"Cooper was not the same for a long time after that. He barely spoke to anyone. He abandoned his weapons training, returning to the workshop where he buried himself in his work. And he refused to see Princess Ashley, blaming both her and himself for John's death. He knew at the time that her decision to enter the thicket was rash, and he did nothing to stop her. He also knew that John was far better at magic than he was with a sword. He never had a chance.

"A healer was assigned the task of visiting your grandfather every day and checking on his wounds.

That's when he met Princess Anna. . She was doing her training with the healer, and she came along as his assistant every day. Anna was quiet and gentle and very different than Ashley. Every day, while she examined his injuries and changed the dressings on his wounds, she talked to him, even when he refused to talk back. She slowly coaxed him back out of the shell he had created for himself, and she helped him find peace and calm again.

"Your grandfather eventually forgave Ashley and returned to fight alongside her during the Gremlin War, but any attraction between them was lost. When the war was over, he returned to Anna. . They carried on a very quiet relationship for a time, but King Marinus didn't like that any better than when your grandfather was seeing Princess Ashley. He thought that Anna was too young and naïve and Cooper was taking advantage of her gentle nature. The king had no choice but to treat him well in public because he was one of the heroes of the Gremlin War, but privately, he still harbored a lot of distrust toward humans. Eventually, Cooper came to the conclusion that he was never going to be accepted by the king, and he wanted to return home. He knew that Anna would insist on coming with him, but he couldn't ask her to abandon her entire world. Then one day, Ged, a gnome scout that your grandfather had befriended during the war, happened to tell him of the Gnome Door and that the current guardian was in failing health. At the time, the Gnome Door was built into an old oak tree hidden in the woods. It seemed like the ideal solution to his problem. They could build a home, move the portal a short distance and live in his world while still keeping contact with this world. Anna could return and visit any time she wished. He petitioned King Marinus to appoint him the new guardian. After considerable prodding from Anna's mother, the queen, who didn't want to lose her daughter forever, the king reluctantly agreed. Secretly, the king assumed that Anna would tire of Cooper, become homesick, and return on her own. She never did, and the King blamed Cooper for the fact that he was wrong.

"Your grandmother and my sister Mina did return once, for the queen's funeral. They hid in the back of the crowd, and King Marinus was never told that they were there. In return, Princess Ashley and I were at your grandmother's funeral."

"You were really there at Grandma Anna's funeral?" Susan asked.

"Yes, we made sure that you never saw us, but we were there. You've grown a bit since then. Now, it's two years later. Anna is gone. Both Ashley and your grandfather are older and wiser, and they seem to have rediscovered the spark between them."

"But my grandmother was her sister," Susan said.

"Yes, she was," Cora answered. "And in human society that might be considered inappropriate. Elven society is a little different. We all loved Anna and will always cherish our memories of her. We also know that she would want both of them to be happy. She was never jealous or selfish, and I'm sure that your grandfather wouldn't do anything that he felt would be disrespectful towards her."

"Okay," Susan said. "I think I understand."

Bodkin was leading the group, anxious to see her brother, when Cora suddenly put a hand to her temple and called for everyone to stop.

"Proceed carefully," she warned. "Something here is terribly wrong."

The closer they got to Pen's campsite, the more concerned they became. To the casual observer, the hillside looked completely ordinary. But to the small group of travelers, something clearly was not right. It was too quiet. No birds chirped, and the usual forest sounds were still. There was no sign of the cave entrance that marked this side of the Gnome Door, and neither Pen nor any of his fellow wardens were anywhere in sight.

They approached cautiously. Bodkin had an arrow knocked on her bow while Cooper, Korin, and the elf guards fanned out and scoured the hillside for some indication of where Pen and his companions might be. Ashley stayed next to Cora and Susan, but her hand was on the hilt of her long knife

A rustle behind them brought them all about with their weapons drawn.

"Oh, Mr. Cooper. Thank the stars that you're here."

It was Mina, but this was not the sweet old housekeeper that Susan was used to. This Mina was dressed in the green of a forest warden and looked like an older version of Bodkin as she moved quickly and efficiently, with just a slight limp. This wasn't the slow moving Mina with the bad foot. Her hair was pulled back, fully revealing her pointed ears. On each hip, she wore a long knife, identical to the ones the princess carried.

Susan was stunned to see this version of Mina. Cooper never even blinked as he asked, "Mina, what's happened here? Do you know where Pen is?"

"He's this way. Quickly, come with me," Mina answered.

Mina led them to a small makeshift shelter hidden among the trees. Pen was lying on a mat and looked barely alive. Bodkin raced over and knelt beside him.

There were tears running down Bodkin's cheeks as Mina came over and put a hand on her shoulder. "Don't cry, child. His fever broke this morning, and I believe the infection is out of his system. The worst is behind him. He has some other injuries, but he'll recover with a little time. I'm afraid that I can't say the same for his two companions," she said as she nodded toward two ominous looking rock piles at the edge of the clearing.

"Was he able to tell you what happened, Mina?" Cooper asked.

Mina nodded. "He's been in and out of delirium due to the fever, but I believe that I've been able to piece most of the story together. They were ambushed. Pen had gone down to the stream to get some water. On his way back, he just sensed that something wasn't right, so he approached quietly, all the time telling himself that it was just his imagination. When he got close enough to see the camp through the trees, he saw that his friends were already down and it was too late for him to help them. They were already being torn apart by wild dogs. They had never even gotten the chance to draw their weapons. Calling up what magic he knew, he sent a ball of brilliant white light into the clearing, exploding it when it reached the center of the pack and blinding the dogs. He was able to kill three of the dogs with his long knife before they could recover. The two remaining dogs were still disoriented and partially blinded, but the larger of the two dogs realized that it could still smell him. Relying on its nose, it leapt straight at Pen. He managed to get his long knife in front of him a split second before the animal struck, and the beast impaled his own throat on the narrow blade. As the dog struck, Pen's foot caught on a root and the impact carried him to the ground with the dog's bulk shattering his arm and snapping off the blade. By the time Pen was able to untangle himself from the carcass, the last dog had recovered from the flash and was on him. With one arm broken and his blade useless, Pen grabbed his talisman with his good hand and called up the magic once more as he rammed his fist into the dog's snapping jaws, incinerating the beast from the inside out. A moment later, as he was dragging himself back to his feet, he was struck from behind.

"He woke up twenty minutes later lying next to the remains of the last dog. He was alive, but one arm was broken and the other was torn up pretty badly from the dog's teeth. He knew from his training that these were nightshade dogs, and even though their bite contained no venom, their saliva was so foul and so contaminated that even a small wound would quickly become infected.

"He had only been unconscious for a few minutes, but he could already feel the fever starting to take hold.

Fortunately, Wysp was nearby and Pen quickly sent her to find me before he slipped into delirium.

"When Wysp suddenly appeared in front of me in middle of the kitchen, I knew something terrible had happened. As soon as Wysp told me about Pen, Cookie and I immediately went out to check on the Gnome Door. We found that the workshop had been ransacked and the intruder already gone. I contacted the neighbors to watch Cookie, grabbed my healing supplies, and came through the door, sealing it from this side like you taught me. Then I moved Pen to this hidden shelter in case his attacker was still nearby, watching the camp."

"Thank you, Mina. That was a wise precaution to seal the door," Cooper said. "Whoever it was must have come back through after they couldn't find what they were looking for but, at least for now, they're contained on this side of the door."

"What could anyone from this world possibly want from your workshop, Mr. Cooper?" asked Mina with a puzzled look on her face.

"I've been secretly guarding an amberstone for many years," Cooper replied. "I'm sorry, I should have confided in you long ago, but I believed that the less people that knew about it, the safer it was. They couldn't find it because I took it with us. But how could anyone know where to look for it? Until Susan stumbled upon it, no one else even knew that it existed."

"The mudwump!" Susan shouted. "When Bodkin and I fought the mudwump, I had to use the amberstone to capture him. He was looking right at the stone as he came towards me."

Cooper nodded, "I think you may be right, Susan. I knew that it was odd to find one of those creatures so far from the swamp. Now I'm sure that it was no accident that he found his way to the Gnome Door. Someone suspected that a stone still existed, and they sent the mudwump in search of it, hoping that the creature's attraction to magic would draw it to the stone."

"And you suspect that it was the same person who imprisoned Prax?" the princess asked.

Cooper turned to the princess. "It has to be. You need to return to the castle immediately. Marinus needs to be told."

"What about you?" Ashley asked.

"I'll have to go find Horus. I have no other choice."

"That crazy old wizard? Is that wise?" Ashley asked, skeptically. "No one really knows where he is, and chances are that if you can find him, he'll do more harm than good."

"Yes, I know. He has become rather eccentric," Cooper answered with a nod. "But he's all that's left of the Guild of Conjurors, and he was very powerful at one time, second only to Eldred. Like it or not, we need him for Susan and I to get home. He was one of my mentors many years ago. I hope that he still remembers me and that I can persuade him to help. I have an idea where I might be able to find him."

"Then I'm coming with you," Ashley said. "Traveling alone, Korin can return to the castle in half the time it would take for all of us to get there. Cora can remain here with my guards and help care for Pen until Korin can return with a patrol. The girls can stay here with her."

Cooper shook his head. "No, Susan comes with us. I swore to her mother that I would keep her close to me and protect her. I wish there was a better solution, but there isn't. Her ability to use red magic may help persuade Horus to assist us."

"Hey, I'm coming too," Bodkin chimed in. "You're not leaving me behind. Pen is in good hands, and I'm not missing out on meeting that old wizard. And I can take care of myself."

The look on the princess's face said no, but Cooper smiled at the princess and pointed out, "Well.....she is very good with that bow. She almost beat you in your little contest."

Ashley sighed. "All right, she can come."

"Good," Cooper said. "We'll get water and some supplies from Pen's camp, and we can leave within the hour."

Chapter 6

A warm breeze was blowing across the hill as Cooper, Princess Ashley, and the two girls left the small makeshift camp by the Gnome Door and started off to find the old wizard. Mina and her twin sister stayed behind to tend to Pen and wait for Korin's return.

"Will they be safe if we leave, Grandfather?" Susan asked.

"They should be. Mina may not be as young as she was once, but she's still very resourceful. She wasn't just your grandmother's nurse. When they were younger, she was also her bodyguard. It was a secret practice of the royal family to train girls in the fighting arts and place them in the castle once they reached a certain age. Assassins never expect ladies in waiting to be trained fighters. One night, three mercenaries scaled the south wall of the castle, killed four guards, and attempted to murder the royal family. Mina found and stopped all three before they could complete their mission. The second one got off a lucky shot, and she was forced to kill the last one with a broken off arrow still sticking out of her leg. That's why she limps. The third assassin almost succeeded. He managed to get close enough to stab your grandmother in the side. It was a minor wound, but the blade was dipped in poison. Mina carried her down to the courtyard and persuaded Prax to fly her to the Healer's Hall, where they had an antidote for the poison. We owe your grandmother's life to Prax and Mina. That's one of the reasons why I couldn't refuse to take the time to look for him."

"I can hardly believe that that was our dear, sweet Mina when I saw her today. And she was barely limping."

"Yes, the healers gave her a special root that she can chew on. It takes the pain away."

"But I've seen her at home. Some days she can hardly walk, especially when it rains. Why doesn't she use the root all the time?"

"Because she knows what would happen. The more you use it, the more you want to use it. After a time, nothing else in your life matters. And it slowly destroys you from within. She would rather limp than allow her life to be controlled by a root."

As they neared the base of the hill, Cooper said, "We'll head southeast, toward the river Equus."

"The Equus?" Ashley asked. Her surprise was obvious from her expression. "That's the boundary to gnome territory. Are you sure that we want to go that way? We won't find very many friendly faces there. After the last flu outbreak, the gnomes aren't very trusting of either humans or elves."

Cooper nodded in agreement. "Yes, there are some long-standing grudges among the gnomes, but I believe that I still have a few friends in that area. There is a small number of gnomes who still use the portal from time to time, and we maintain an amicable relationship. Also, there's not a lot of settlements along the river; it tends to flood too often. With a little luck, we may avoid contact altogether. Years ago, Horus kept a small cabin hidden along the banks of the Equus. I know that he chose that location deliberately to avoid visitors. He surrounded it with a spell that makes trespassers become confused and lose their way if they come too close. Of course, he considers everyone to be a trespasser, but I think I remember how to counter his protective spell if I can just get us close enough to find the cabin."

The small group hiked silently for the next hour as the terrain slowly turned hillier, with denser patches of forest.

They had just left a thick stand of old growth oaks when the sound of movement from behind them brought them to a halt.

Creatures began to appear from all sides. They were nightshade dogs, nearly twenty in the pack, and they were heading straight for the group of travelers at a casual lope. Nightshade dogs, demonic cousins of coyotes, the same creatures that attacked Pen and his companions. They had a ridge of black spikey fur running down their backbone, and they had long, yellow teeth. Nightshade dogs weren't quite as big as wolves, but they were just as vicious. They normally hunted at dusk and avoided people. It was unusual to see them out in the open at this time of day.

The group was completely exposed, almost in the center of the clearing, and the dogs were spreading out as they came, clearly trying to encircle them. Any attempt to retreat into the relative safety of the trees was instantly cut off.

Cooper's staff flared bright as he burned two of the lead creatures, but as soon as he focused his fire in one direction, the animals on the opposite side instantly started to close in. Bodkin managed to put an arrow into the side of one of the dogs, but that wasn't enough to incapacitate it, and the wounded creature just moved to the outer edge of the circle. Realizing that her arrows wouldn't stop the creatures, Bodkin put her last arrow into the left eye of the closest one. It ran off shrieking in pain. The pack continued to slowly circle closer and closer, looking for the opportunity to rush the group.

As Cooper and Ashley defended from the right, one of the dogs on the left broke from the line and charged straight at Susan. The small talisman from around her neck was already clenched tightly in her hand as she desperately tried to call up some magic that would stop the dog, but the tiny bit of stone remained dull and lifeless as the dog raced toward her with bared teeth and claws.

An instant before the creature could strike, a bolt of blue shot out from among the trees and slammed into the dog with the force of a sledgehammer. The impact catapulted the dog backwards into the pack, scattering the other creatures. The momentary confusion allowed Cooper to focus on the three closest nightshade dogs, and he burned them to ashes as the unseen figure from the trees continued the assault from the flank.

Caught in the crossfire, a dozen of the creatures were rapidly dispatched. The two-sided onslaught was more than the dogs expected, and what remained of the pack quickly broke off the attack and headed for the protection of the forest. In less than a minute, they were gone.

The acrid smell of burnt fur hung in the air as the group turned to see two figures emerge from the edge of the trees. Susan was the first to recognize them.

"Mom! Grandfather, look, it's Mom!"

Susan was right. It was her mother, Elana, who had saved them. She came across the clearing at a run and scooped up Susan in her arms.

In between hugs, Elana said, "When Wysp came to me, I knew that it meant trouble and that I had to come. She told me that you were trapped here. Is anyone hurt?"

"No, we're all fine, thanks to you," Cooper answered. "How did you find us?"

"Wysp was able to follow the traces of magic. She led us right to you," Elana answered as she set Susan down and hugged her father. "Dad, I'm so glad that everyone is okay." Then she slapped her father hard across the shoulder. "But dammit, Dad, you promised me that this would just be a quiet weekend hike." Before Cooper even had the chance to respond, Elana turned on the princess. "And you, Aunt Ashley, just *once* I'd like to come here without you being up to your pointed ears in trouble. You attract it like a magnet, and you drag everyone around you into it with you. You may still be able to charm my dad, but if anything had happened to Susan, I'd be tearing those big blue eyes out right about now."

Ashley stood her ground, but her voice was cold as ice. "Always the lady. Just as I remember. It's nice to see you, too, Elana. Thank you for your timely help, and I assure you, I wouldn't allow any harm to come to my favorite niece, Susan."

Before the two women had the chance to say any more, Cooper stepped between them. "I truly am sorry, Elana. I did intend for this to just be a simple trip, but you know firsthand that things here don't always go as planned. Mina said that she sealed the Gnome Door. Even I can't open it from this side once it's been sealed. How were you able to get here?"

"I had to call in a couple of favors." Elana motioned to the silent figure that still hung in the shadows near the trees. Cooper's face lit up as he recognized the old elf that shuffled forward.

"Quisp, you old dog, I should have guessed that you'd still know a secret passage to the other world. But I was told that you had been lost in the Gremlin Wars. How did you survive?"

"A simple deception, My Lord," Quisp answered. "A new location and a new name. Not very difficult after the confusion following an invasion. I'm sure you recall that our old location was not that far from gremlin lands. We made more than a few enemies among those friendly to the gremlins. I had no desire to have my throat slit while I slept. No one comes to try and kill you if they believe that you're already dead, though it did break my heart to have to abandon the old Dragon's Breath."

"And your brother?" Cooper asked.

"Gone, Sir. When the gremlin forces approached, he stayed behind to delay the invaders and ensure that all the innocents escaped. He was the only one left in the village when it was overrun," Quisp said sadly.

"Noble to the end. He was a fine elf, and I was privileged to call him my friend," Cooper said. "If I had known that you were still alive, I would have sought you out. It seems that my daughter is also good at keeping secrets. Your presence creates a dilemma, though. It provides us with a way home, but it also offers an unguarded passage for our unknown enemy to escape into our world."

"The passage is buried deep in the labyrinths of the Ice Caves," Quisp answered. "No one will stumble upon it by accident."

"It's well hidden, Dad," Elana spoke up. "We can take you there. C'mon, let's get to a less exposed spot in case those dogs decide to come back. Then we can plan how to proceed."

Cooper agreed, and the travelers quickly moved to a protected spot among a stand of tall maples to plan. After a short discussion, it was decided they would all go into the Ice Caves to ensure that Susan and Elana safely reached the portal and were on their way home. Then Cooper and Ashley would resume their trek to find the old wizard and somehow persuade him to return with them to restore the Gnome Door. Quisp and Bodkin would return to the camp near the Gnome Door where the twin sisters cared for Bodkin's brother.

Susan's mind raced as they started out. The Spirit of the Golden Willow's warning was that both she and Bodkin needed to stay near her grandfather, but they were all splitting up soon. She knew that she had to be very careful who she revealed her secrets to, but she was going to have to tell someone before she passed through the portal. Once she was on the other side, she couldn't help her grandfather and, if the spirit was correct, the results could be disastrous. Susan trusted the spirit, but she just didn't see how she would be of any real help. Her grandfather was very good at magic and, earlier, when the dogs had tried to attack her, she couldn't make the magic work even to save herself. At least that was something she could ask her grandfather about and maybe she would find out something useful that would help her convince her mother and grandfather that she needed to stay.

When they came upon a stream of crystal clear water after about an hour, Cooper suggested a ten minute rest to refill their canteens, and Susan saw an opportunity to ask about the magic. She quickly moved to sit next to him.

"Grandfather, I'm confused. When the dogs attacked us, I couldn't make the magic work, just like when the mudwump was in your workshop. But both you and Mom were able to destroy the dogs with magic. I was able to free Prax with red magic, so why does it work differently for me?"

Cooper sighed. "I didn't lie to you when I said that you couldn't use the magic to destroy or harm anything. I meant that you wouldn't be able to do that without being trained. There is a good reason why you cannot use magic in that way and I hoped that you would never need to. Magic is part of the individual person's nature, and harming or destroying another living thing is not a natural act. You use your talisman to focus it, but the magic must come from within you. Before you can use the darker side of magic, you need to be carefully trained. Such use requires you to tap into the least desirable parts of your personality, and each time you do, you lose a tiny piece of yourself. It chips away at your soul, and even experienced magic users can be overwhelmed by darkness."

"But, Grandfather, you can do it and you're not mean or evil. You're the kindest and gentlest person I know," Susan said.

"With time and practice, you can restore balance and send the demons of your mind back to where they belong. Your grandmother helped me to learn that," Cooper answered. "But just as the magic that you've done up to now has required you to focus your thoughts on calm pleasant things, destruction requires you to focus on darker things like anger, fear, and especially hatred. Everyone possesses these qualities, and most of us try to keep them under control. Before a person can use magic in that way, they must go through a special process known as the kuri-aken, and it needs to be done under the strictest supervision.

"The princess and I both went through the ritual at the Hall of Conjurers before it was destroyed, and I can assure you that it is not a pleasant process. The guild monitored every student carefully before allowing them to become a candidate, and no one under the age of sixteen was even allowed to try. The ritual requires you to go deep inside your subconscious mind where all of your worst fears and anxieties are buried. Your mind must travel through the parts of the dreamscape where all of your worst nightmares exist, and you can experience many of them all at once. Through the process, you must learn to use those dark qualities and still be able to return them to the dark recesses of your mind when you no longer need them. Without a trained observer, the candidates can easily get lost in their own fears and go completely insane. More than one candidate has become trapped in the frightening world of their own subconscious and never recovered.

"When your mother was sixteen, she spent most of her summer vacation at Kestriana and, with the help of the princess and a few others, we trained her to do magic. She was a good student and a natural at magic. By the end of the summer, your mother was eligible to be a candidate. Horus was the only observer who still remained. Most of the guild members were killed when the hall was destroyed, but old Horus was away from the hall that day and he survived. He had grown old and more than a little eccentric, and he had become a bit of a recluse who only traveled to the castle once a year to perform the ritual. I arrived at the castle ten minutes after the process was scheduled to begin and discovered that

Horus had been delayed and wasn't there yet. Knowing that your mother could be headstrong and impulsive, I suspected that she might become just impatient enough to foolishly try to begin the process on her own. We raced to the exam room and discovered that I had guessed correctly. We arrived just two minutes after she had started. We found her curled up in the far corner of the room, shrieking. It took two weeks to calm her to the point that she could sleep for more than an hour at a time without horrible nightmares, and it was six months until she was back to her old self. Your grandmother nearly strangled both of us and wouldn't allow her to come back here for over a year. It also required a lot of persuasion to convince old Horus to allow her to attempt it again.

"Finally, a year and a half later, she was given permission to try again. This time, she waited very patiently for Horus to arrive, followed his instructions exactly, and got through the whole ritual without incident."

Elana came up behind Cooper just as he was finishing. "Yes, I did. That was a painful lesson to learn. Sorry for snapping at you earlier, Dad. I was just so worried that something terrible would happen to the two of you before we could get here."

She motioned to Quisp, and the old elf approached. "Susan, this is Quisp. I didn't have a chance to properly introduce him earlier. He's mine and your grandfather's old friend, and he's going to lead us back through the Ice Caves so we can get home.

"I am at your service, Princess," Quisp said, bowing from the waist.

"But I'm not a princess," Susan answered.

"Forgive me, but your grandmother was the king's daughter. That makes you a princess," Quisp insisted.

"Don't bother arguing with him, Susan," Elana said. "I tried to get him to stop calling me that for years, and he just won't listen."

"Well, okay, it's nice to meet you, anyway," Susan responded. "Will it be cold in the Ice Caves, Mr. Quisp?"

"No, little princess. There is no real ice in the caves. The 'ice' is made up of hundreds of clear crystals that line the walls. Even Wysp and her fairy friends don't know how they came to be there. The crystals glow with an ever-changing light that sparkles and flickers and sometimes can be as bright as midday. So bright, in fact, that early on, elves had no fear of the caves, as they naturally would if they were dark. But they soon discovered that there are far worse things in the Ice Caves to fear than the dark. The crystals can be mesmerizing to look at. When the caves were first found, many folks came to marvel at their beauty. They soon realized that the caves form a labyrinth, some say an enchanted labyrinth. Dozens of people went in and never returned. Did they just became so hopelessly lost that they eventually died trying to find a way out and their bones still lie in the caves where they fell? No one knows.

"Entire search parties were sent in and lost. Engineers were brought in to try to map the caves, and they, too, were lost. Rumors began to spread about horrible beasts living deep in the caves and luring victims in with the light from the crystals, but no evidence of any beast was ever found. Finally, the entrance was sealed, but there are those who believe that the crystals were put there by an ancient wizard to guard a great treasure hidden at the heart of the maze. Every year, treasure seekers will come and unseal the entrance. They always believe that the earlier explorers were fools, but they will be the ones smart enough to defeat the crystals and solve the mystery of the labyrinth. Most times, they never return from their search. When I was much younger, I, too, was fool enough to believe the stories of treasure. Why else would the crystals exist if not to protect something of great value? I barely escaped with my life. My companions were not so lucky. Only a small handful of people have ever found their way in and out. You must stick to a certain path or be lost forever. I know of only one safe passage that leads to a portal to your world, and I will only go there in a dire emergency. When we reach the caves, do not wander off, little princess. Your very life depends on it." An hour later, they approached the entrance to the Ice Caves. Large stones that had, at one time, sealed the entrance were scattered about, and there was an opening large enough for them to enter one at a time. Many of the stones had dire warnings etched into them. Some were written in the flowing elven script and others in the bold block lettering of the gnome language. All of them were ominous.

Before entering the caves, Quisp again repeated his warnings. "Stay together and follow exactly where I lead. Do not stray from the path, and do not stare at the lights from the crystals. They will confuse and bewitch your mind. There will be a number of large cavern rooms with many tunnels leading off in all directions. This is where the lights will be the worst and we must be most careful. If we become separated and you go down the wrong tunnel, there is little chance that we will be able to find you."

At Quisp's direction, Elana took the lead and set off down one of the smaller corridors on the right. The lights blinked and sparkled, and both Susan and Bodkin carefully followed Quisp's warnings not to stare at them. Cooper and Quisp brought up the rear, and the group passed through a half dozen small rooms with numerous exits; each time, Quisp pointed out which route they needed to take.

All sense of time was quickly lost until, finally, after what seemed like hours of wandering down twisting and turning corridors, Quisp announced that there was only one more large room they had to pass through to reach the last tunnel that would take them to their destination; but they had to remain focused on passing through quickly, as this room would be the worst one that they would encounter.

As they entered the room, it quickly became clear that Quisp was not exaggerating. The cavern was dazzling. Light shining from the ceiling made stalactites look like enormous chandeliers. Massive columns glowed as the light played up and down in varying hues. The walls were alive with moving colors. It sparkled like a giant banquet hall set up for the grandest of all grand balls. The entire group let out a collective gasp as they entered the shimmering room.

"Look at the floor and at the feet of the person in front of you!" Quisp cried. As soon as they were all looking down, he led them as quickly as possible across the cavernous room to a doorway on the far side.

They were almost through the great room when a cloaked figure suddenly bolted out of one of the small tunnel entrances to their right. With his hood pulled up, his face was completely obscured. He froze in his tracks when he saw the band of travelers.

Cooper had moved to the front of the group, on the lookout for any unfriendly cave-dwelling creatures that they might encounter lurking in the tunnel entrance. A hooded figure was not what he was expecting, but he was quick to recover from the surprise and he immediately extended his hand in a universal gesture of friendship.

The hooded figure wasn't interested in being friendly. The stranger's dark staff, the top of which was carved into the shape of a dragon, instantly began to glow bright blue. His intent was immediately clear.

"Run!" Cooper shouted. "Into the tunnel, everyone!" He didn't know who the stranger was, but the fact that he carried a staff showed that he possessed considerable skill at magic and fully intended to unleash the full fury of it against them. The girls sprinted for the tunnel entrance with Quisp bringing up the rear as Cooper hoped that he would be able to at least deflect the blast of magic that he knew would be coming.

An instant before the attack came, a second figure, a woman this time, darted out of another one of the entrances from across the room. Moving fast and staying low, she threw her own bolt of magic at the hooded figure as she came.

The two magics collided with a blast that shook the entire cave like a small earthquake and caused all the crystals to go dark. Cooper hunched down behind his own shield of magic and, in the split second before a cloud of smoke and dust obscured both the room and the first fifty yards of the corridor, he caught a glimpse of the witch as the force of the explosion knocked her from her feet and hurled her across the room like a rag doll. She had had no time to protect herself while attacking the cloaked figure. For what seemed like an eternity, the group huddled together in the corridor, unable to move through the blinding cloud and the pitch dark. When the dust finally began to clear enough to see more than a few inches and a small number of crystals began to wink back on, Cooper discovered that Quisp was no longer with them. He prayed that he would not find Quisp's crumpled body on the other side of the tunnel entrance.

They found him alive and unharmed in the big room. The cloaked wizard was gone, and Quisp knelt next to the witch who was crumpled on the floor. Quisp sat beside her, holding her head in his lap. Tears ran freely down his face.

As the others approached, he pleaded with them. "Please, help her.... She's a...friend."

Bodkin was the first to respond. "Help her? Have you lost your mind? Leave her and let's get out of here before that wizard, or whoever he was, comes back. At the very least we should go before she wakes up and tries to kill us all again. She's a witch, and everyone knows that witches hate elves."

"No, you're wrong about her," Quisp cried. "She saved my life. Cooper, you've had training as a healer. Please, you must help her. The rest of you can go on. The way is straight ahead. But I won't abandon her."

"I'll stay and do what I can for her," Cooper said. "Ashley, get everyone else out of here. We'll catch up as soon as we can."

Ashley hesitated for a moment then pulled Cooper aside and quietly asked, "Cooper, Bodkin is right. She is a witch. No witches have been seen for decades, but they always were the traditional enemies of the elves. She may very well try to kill both of you the instant that she opens her eyes. You would be taking quite a risk. Is it wise to try and help her?"

"Probably not, but I saw what happened and Quisp is telling the truth. She could have easily stayed hidden in that tunnel and we would never have known that she was there. If she had only wanted to harm that wizard, she could easily have ambushed him after he attacked us. She took a big risk exposing herself to save Quisp. Everyone else was already safely in the corridor, but he was the last in line and too far away for the shield I threw up to protect him. That blast would have killed him if she hadn't tried to block it. Now, please get the rest to safety. I'm trusting you and Elana to work together to keep Susan and Bodkin safe until we can catch up."

Cooper knelt and began to examine the witch's injuries while Ashley reluctantly led the rest of the group down the corridor. As soon as the others were gone, Cooper spoke to Quisp.

"I didn't want to say anything in front of the two girls, but you're asking me to take a lot on faith, old friend," Cooper said. "If you get me killed, I guarantee you that both Ashley and Elana will track you down and cut off your pointed ears. I've always known that you associated with some unsavory characters, but a witch? And you called her a *friend*? You had better have a good explanation for this one."

Quisp shook his head. "I'll tell you everything I know if you just help her."

Cooper sighed as he handed Quisp a clean cloth from his pack. "I've already said that I would help her. I'll do everything that I can. Clean some of the dust off her face while I check to see if any bones are broken."

Quisp carefully wiped her face as he began. "Her name is Shirell. It was many years ago, not long after the war ended, when she came to the new pub very late one night. It was long after everyone else had gone home, and I was just puttering around, doing a little cleaning behind the bar. I wasn't sleeping much back then. I guess I was still having some trouble getting used to the idea that my brother, the old pub, and most of the people that I had known for so many years were all gone. War is a terrible thing, even long after it's over. I had to keep telling myself that Quark wasn't just in the back room, counting the inventory or putting away supplies. Or maybe just off doing any one of the other countless things that we did at the pub.

"There was a terrible storm blowing outside, and I must have had the only light on for miles around. I thought I heard a faint knock on the door, so I stopped what I was doing and listened. After a minute, I heard it again. Someone was at the door. I wasn't sure if I wanted to take a chance opening it that late at night. There were still individuals out there who knew my real identity and my actions during the war. Some of them wouldn't hesitate to remove one troublesome elf from their world. But it could also have been some lost traveler who got caught in the storm. For some unknown reason, I decided to risk it and opened the door warily, my long knife concealed behind the door but ready in my hand.

"She stood before me, huddled in the doorway, her ragged cloak pulled up over her head to protect her from the storm. She looked up at me with dark eyes. There was a sad loneliness in those eyes. A desperate need for a bit of kindness. There was also something there that was frightening, a hollow blackness behind her eyes that seemed to bore right into your soul. Part of me wanted to slam the door closed and bar it shut, but how could I turn her away? She was barely a girl and she was cold, wet, and looked half dead from the storm, and except for the hollow eyes, she didn't appear to pose any sort of a threat. I think that she just wanted someplace warm to get out of the storm. So I left her in. I still had some soup on the stove that I had been keeping warm, hoping that it would help me get to sleep. I gave her a blanket and some soup and had her sit by the hearth and dry off. She didn't speak, and after a bit I realized that I was talking enough for both of us. I don't really know why. She didn't make any attempt to stop me, so I just chattered on while I continued to clean up the pub. She seemed lonely, and maybe I was, too.

"She went through two bowls of soup as if she hadn't eaten in a week. She still looked hungry so, on a whim, I offered her some chocolate that I had brought back from the human world. She eyed it suspiciously at first, but once she tried a small taste of it, she seemed to like it.

"After she had dried off and warmed up a bit, she looked a lot less frightening. So I showed her to the small spare room in the back where she could sleep if she wished, or at least wait until the storm passed. I showed her how to bar the door from the inside so no one else could get in and she would be safe. Then I said goodnight and went to bed myself. When I looked in on her the next morning, she was gone.

"I had almost forgotten about her until a month later when I heard a gentle knock on the pub door late one night. She had come back. I invited her in and asked if perhaps she would like some soup and maybe just a little chocolate. She nodded, and I gave her a little of both. She stayed for about an hour while I cleaned the pub, and she listened silently while I told her about the evening's events. Then she quietly got up, went to the door, and said 'Goodnight, Elf,' and vanished into the night.

"Those were the first words that she had ever spoken to me and the way she said 'elf' made it clear that she was not fond of my kind.

"Sometimes she would come back on the night of the new moon, when it was darkest, without any moonlight. Other times, I wouldn't see her for months. Then, suddenly, she would reappear. It was always the same routine. She would sit by the hearth and listen silently while I told her all the latest news and rumors. She rarely stayed more than an hour. Sometimes she would decline the bowl of soup, but she always accepted the offer of a bit of chocolate. And she never spoke more than just to say, 'Goodnight, Elf.'

"I had stumbled upon her weakness. She had a sweet tooth for chocolate. I began to keep a regular supply, replenishing it any time that I slipped through the fairy mists into the human world. It took quite some time, and a lot of chocolate, until she finally started to talk to me.

"There was one night with no moon and a few clouds blotting out the stars. It was as black as the inside of a cave. I just somehow knew that she would be coming that night. It was only a short time after closing that I heard a familiar faint knock at the door. I left her in as usual. Over time, she had become far different then when I had met her. She was no longer the half drowned bit of a girl that she had been on that first night. I had been around magic users before, and I knew the signs. She moved soundlessly, like a wraith, and even though I trusted that she would not harm me, deep inside I was still a bit frightened. When I offered her something to eat, she declined with a nod of her head. Then I offered her the usual bit of chocolate and, for the first time, I saw a glimpse of a smile.

"As she accepted the chocolate she said, 'Thank you, Quisp. You're very kind...for an elf.'

"It was the first time that she had ever spoken my name, and I hadn't called myself 'Quisp' since the end of the war.

"'Some of my kind have been cruel to you, haven't they?' I asked.

"She nodded, and there was a spark of fire in her eyes when she quietly said, 'More than you can imagine, but you're different. Whenever I come here, you tell me all about what's going on in the area. You have been my eyes and ears in the community. Some of that information has been very helpful. You know what I am and that I could cause great harm with some of that information, and yet you trust me. I promise you that I have never used anything that you've told me to harm any of your friends. You've been very trusting and open with me. I think that you've earned a bit of my trust. Come and sit across from me, bring that wonderful chocolate with you, and let me tell you a little about elf cruelty.' Then she spent the next hour telling me who she was and how she came to be there.

"She began by telling me that she was born in one of the small farming villages that dotted the border. Her mother's family belonged to one of the small groups of humans that had stumbled into this world generations ago and made it their home. At a very early age, she exhibited a talent for magic. When she began to move objects and charm small animals, her mother, Kiri, quickly realized that she was special. Kiri couldn't do magic herself. That skill had come from Shirell's father. Shirell had never met her father.

"Kiri had told her the story many times about the handsome young elf named Brin who had come to work on their farm one summer. Brin was apprenticed to the Hall of Conjurors and had shown great promise, but they had no space for him until the end of summer. So he was sent to work at Kiri's family's farm to help pay for his room and board at the hall, and after the harvest, he would begin his apprenticeship full time. Brin was quickly smitten with the pretty young human girl with the dark eyes and he would perform small tricks to entertain her. Early on, Kiri had ignored him, thinking that he was brash and arrogant. But he was able to slowly win her over, and by the end of the summer, Kiri and Brin were in love. They spent his last night at the farm together.

"Early the next morning, Brin left for the Hall of Conjurors, promising to return for her when his training was complete. Before he left, he gave Kiri a pendant as a token of his love. The pendant contained a small piece of amberstone. A month later, Kiri and her family received a message saying that Brin had never arrived at the hall. Brin had disappeared without a trace and was never found or heard from again."

"I remember hearing the story about Brin's disappearance when I was at the hall," Cooper said. "There was great concern that such a promising young talent had just vanished off the face of the earth."

Quisp nodded as he continued. "By the time that she turned twelve, Shirell had discovered her talents and was secretly borrowing her mother's pendant and experimenting on her own. One day, when she was fifteen, despite her mother's warnings, she tried to use magic to move an old stump at the far end of the meadow. The magic got out of control, and the explosion threw Shirell fifty feet through the air and set the neighbor's barn on fire. After that, Kiri knew that Shirell needed training that she wasn't able to provide so she sent a message to the Hall of Conjurors. It was unusual for the hall to accept a girl that young into their apprentice program, but when they were told that she was Brin's daughter, they agreed to train her.

"When Shirell received the news that she had been accepted at the hall, she was ecstatic. The opportunity to study and practice openly was something that she had long dreamed about. Most of the villagers that lived nearby were human farmers and were fearful of magic and its use, so she had always had to practice in secret.

Being a half-elf, she had always been a bit of a misfit among both the humans and the local elves. She was tolerated, but not really accepted in either group. At the hall, she would be accepted for who she was and be able to do magic. It was everything that she had ever wished for. She was so excited that she packed her few belongings, said goodbye to Kiri, and left that very afternoon. She traveled all night, arriving at the hall unexpectedly the next morning. She was shown to a room by an old servant. The headmaster and all the instructors were all still at breakfast.

"Sadly, she had arrived on the worst day imaginable. Twenty minutes later, while she was still unpacking her belongings, the hall was attacked by the lindworm. She was trapped inside when the building collapsed, and the only person who knew that she was in the hall was killed in the attack. Because the room that the old man had put her in was at the far wing of the hall, she was saved from the worst of the destruction. She wasn't badly hurt, but she was trapped under a heavy beam. The beam had fallen in such a way that it created a small cavity in the debris, and it had saved her from being crushed by the stones of the building. A tiny opening in the pile of stones allowed her to see out, but she couldn't move or attempt to free herself without bringing a ton of rocks down on top of her.

"She lay trapped there for three days, praying for someone to come and find her. When she finally did hear voices nearby, she wasn't certain if they were real or a hallucination. As she looked out through her tiny peephole, she saw Princess Ashley and her personal guards who had come to examine the damage and report back to the Elven High Council. Shirell could see the princess and tried to call out to her, but by then she was so weak and dehydrated that all she could manage was a feeble cry that went unheard. Ashley and her men had come with a local farmer from the nearby village. The man supplied eggs for the hall and had been on his way to make his delivery that day. The farmer had witnessed the attack from the edge of the woods. The farmer said that he had been terrified and had never seen such utter destruction. He was familiar with the day to day routine at the hall and told them that everyone would have been at breakfast in the main dining room when the attack came. The princess looked at the pile of rubble that had once been the hall and assured the man that there was nothing he could have done to help and that no one could have survived such devastation. The princess and her men walked around the building only once before mounting up and returning to the castle. No one ever looked for survivors, and Shirell was left abandoned in the rubble."

"She can't blame the princess for believing that there were no survivors," Cooper said. "I rode by the hall a week later and saw for myself that the building had been leveled. It's a miracle that anyone could have lived through that."

"I agree. I also saw what remained of the hall," Quisp added. "But that's only part of it. When Kiri received word of the hall's destruction, she sent a frantic message to the castle, pleading with the princess to search for Shirell or to at least send a few men to accompany Kiri while she searched. She got a message a week later saying that the princess was very sorry, but all were lost in the destruction of the hall and, due to the presence of the Gremlin Army, no one could be spared for a search. Kiri was devastated with grief. First she lost Brin, and now Shirell. It was more than she could bear, and she attempted to go to the hall herself and search even though the Gremlin Army was now camped between her village and the hall. She tried to skirt the outer edges of the encampment, but she was a simple farm girl not trained at that sort of thing. She got careless and was captured by a patrol from the Gremlin Army. They hung her on a pole and tortured her for three days before she finally died of exposure. When the gremlins moved on, they left her mangled body hanging there for the birds to pick at."

"That's horrible," Cooper said as he continued to examine the witch. "But how did Shirell escape being buried alive? Someone must have come along and dug her out of the rubble."

"No," Quisp said, shaking his head. "After Princess Ashley left, Shirell knew that she would have to save herself or die there under a ton of debris. She was wearing her mother's pendant around her neck. She had no choice but to use magic to free herself."

"But destroying objects is a difficult task even for a trained magic-wielder," Cooper said. "She hadn't been taught yet."

"Yes, I know of the kuri-aken process and that it must be performed before one can use magic in that way," Quisp answered. "But somehow, alone and trapped under a ton of rocks, she did it."

"Oh my God, she did the kuri-aken all alone?" Cooper stared at Quisp, wide-eyed. "It's incredible that she survived. It's even more amazing that she has any sanity at all after that."

"Some would say that I don't," a feeble voice answered. Both men jumped as the witch's dark eyes flashed open. "Telling stories about me, Quisp? I should have known better than to try to save you, you old fool."

"Please don't be angry with me, Mistress. You were hurt. I couldn't just leave you." Quisp cried.

"Yes, all right.....and haven't I told you before not to call me that? I'm not your mistress." She scolded Quisp with her words, but the tone of her voice held no genuine anger toward the old elf. Shirell turned her dark eyes on Cooper. "You're the human they call Cooper. I have no quarrel with you, but I don't like being touched...or having my life revealed to strangers," she added with a harsh look in Quisp's direction. "I don't believe that anything is broken. I was able to partially shield myself from the blast. Please allow me to sit up." The witch rose to a sitting position and appeared to be fully recovered as she accepted a drink from the water skin that Quisp offered. "I know your reputation for being a good man, so I will repay your kindness by finishing Quisp's story. I trust that you will respect my privacy and not repeat it. Your guess was correct. As soon as I entered the dreamscape, I was overwhelmed by the demons in my mind. My sanity was being torn apart, and I was far too weak and inexperienced to fight them off. I nearly went mad and most certainly would have died screaming, under that pile of rubble. Then a distant voice reached out to me. A lifeline that allowed me to find my way back. The voice claiming to be my flesh and blood come to help me, but my mother knew nothing of magic, and my father died before I was born. Whoever it was slowly coaxed me back from the abyss, helping me to drive the demons back and teaching me how to hold them at bay. Before I awoke, the voice offered me a glimmer of hope on how to escape. It couldn't help me in the real world, but it told me that rather than try to move a ton of rocks above me, I should use the magic to tunnel under the debris. The earth was soft and I was near the outside wall. I was so weak that it took hours, sometimes moving only an inch at a time, constantly stopping to rest. Finally, after almost a day, I dragged myself out of my would-be tomb and escaped."

    Shirell stood and brushed some of the dust from her clothing as she finished her story. "The stories about the caves are only half right. There is no great treasure nor are there any monsters here, but the labyrinth can be deadly. The tunnel ahead will take you where you want to go. Do not stray from the main corridor and do *not* attempt to follow me. Goodbye to both of you." She threw a quick glance at Quisp and muttered, "Troublesome old elf."

    Then in a flash, she disappeared down one of the side tunnels.

Cooper and Quisp stared at the tunnel entrance that the witch had vanished into for a moment before Quisp said, "She's really not so bad once you get to know her."

Cooper just shook his head and smiled as he got to his feet. "Come on then, we need to catch up to the girls."

Cooper and Quisp moved quickly down the tunnel to rejoin the rest of the group. It didn't take them long. Ashley, Elana, and the two girls were already stopped and waiting. The tunnel ahead was blocked and impassable. Quisp would have to lead them back through the caves the way they had come. Now, they had no choice. They would have to go back and find the wizard Horus to unseal the Gnome Door. Susan couldn't help feeling relieved that her own dilemma was solved for the time being.

Chapter 7

Shirell cursed under her breath as she hurried down the tunnel. Her leg hurt terribly, but she had had no intention of letting either Cooper or Quisp know that she was injured. She knew that nothing was broken but it felt like she had been hit with a club.

She was sure that Cooper knew how to use the magic to subdue much of the pain. It was no secret that he was trained as a healer, and under other circumstances, she could have learned a lot from the guardian. But she had no desire to be indebted to Cooper or anyone else. At the moment, Cooper and his family were neither friends nor enemies, and Shirell was content to keep it that way. She didn't know how much she could trust any of them. Her first rule of survival had always been, trust as few people as possible. Best to keep them at arm's length.

Why couldn't the Shadow Mage have come out of that tunnel just one minute later? They would have all been gone by then. Long before she had distanced herself from him, she knew that sooner or later she would have to confront the shadow mage. She had wanted to face him on her own terms. Shirell had never had any real interest in the mage's plans to destroy the Elven High Council and bring down the king. All she ever really wanted was to punish Princess Ashley for what had been done to her mother.

She no longer blamed the princess for her own ordeal. Shirell had long ago accepted the fact that, despite her initial anger toward the princess's unwillingness to search the ruins, the devastation of the Hall of Conjurers was so severe that no one could have expected there to be any survivors. Quisp had been there to see the aftermath and confirmed that there was no way that Princess Ashley or anyone else could have believed that she was still alive under all that rubble. But if the Princess had been willing to spare just one guard or, better still, a warden of the forest to escort her mother safely past the Gremlin Army, Kiri would still be alive. Princess Ashley's refusal to send any help was the one thing that Shirell just could not forgive.

Early on, working together with the shadow mage seemed like it would allow both of them to achieve their objectives, but she soon realized that the mage's plans went far beyond simple revenge. The dark wizard was mad. His insane plans to destroy the king would devastate their entire world, and very possibly the human world also. She had played a dangerous game allowing him to believe that she shared in his hatred while he taught her to use and refine her skills at magic. After today's encounter, the line had been crossed and there would be no going back. She knew far too much about him. The shadow mage would try to kill her on sight. At least she knew which direction the dark wizard was going, and she deliberately chose a different tunnel that would take her the opposite way. One confrontation was enough for today.

Years ago, she had discovered that there was a specific pattern to the labyrinth of the Ice Caves. The reason that so many became lost in the caves was because of a very subtle enchantment placed there by the fairies of old that caused confusion and forgetfulness. The spell would seep so deep into a person's subconscious that only the most experienced magic wielders would notice it, and there were very few of them left. Once you understood the pattern and took a simple precaution to protect yourself from the spell, you could traverse the caves without fear of getting lost.

Finally, the pain in her leg forced her to stop and rest. The instant that she sat down, a weight landed on her shoulder. Startled, she spun to her right and found herself nose to nose with a small furry face. Pinkie! The little snicker had caught up to her. She had had no idea if Pinkie had been present for the fight with the shadow mage, or if he was alive or dead. She reached up and scratched his ears as he rubbed his nose against hers. At least, this was one friend that she could trust. After a short rest, she would follow the tunnel that would take her home. Both Princess Ashley and the shadow mage would have to wait until another day.

The shadow mage seethed with anger. Fate had presented him with the perfect opportunity. Both Princess Ashley and that bothersome human, Cooper, together in the Ice Caves. Just a few more unfortunate victims of the deadly maze. No one would ever risk searching for them in that labyrinth. He could have destroyed them both if not for that ungrateful little witch, Shirell. How dare she oppose him. When he found her, she was living with the nightshade dogs and her skill with magic amounted to little more than charming little forest animals. He had trained and coaxed her along until she was a skilled magic wielder, and she repaid him by running off and abandoning him. The blast in the cave had knocked her clear across the room. She was hurt, he was sure of that. He should have stayed and finished off the miserable little wench, but the blast blew back his hood. He couldn't allow any of them to see his face, not yet. Once he possessed the magical talisman known as the Eye of Bangor Khan, secrecy would no longer matter, and she would regret her foolish actions.

Today's confrontation was only a minor inconvenience. In reality, he wanted Cooper alive. The guardian knew where the eye was hidden, of that the shadow mage was certain. At least Cooper wouldn't be returning home to the human world for a while. The shadow mage had made sure of that when he blocked the tunnel in the Ice Caves. They would need to go and find that crazy old wizard, Horus, if they wanted to return home. And the mage would be waiting for them when they did. Cooper wasn't the only one who knew about the cabin on the river Equus. There were many isolated spots along the way, the mage reminded himself. Unfortunate things can happen to unwary travelers. The next two days were quiet and uneventful as they traveled back toward the river Equus in search of the old wizard. There were small settlements and farms scattered along the way where they were able to get food and supplies.

On the evening of the second day, they set up camp in a small wooded area that offered some protection from the cold night air. Because of their last encounter with the nightshade dogs, the adults took turns keeping watch during the night. Cooper offered to take the first watch.

An hour after everyone had turned in, as he sat watching the flames of the campfire dance, the carving on his staff began to glow faintly. He had sensed Shirell's presence a few hours ago which is why he deliberately took the first watch. He knew that she had been following them at a distance for most of the day, but this was the first time that she had approached.

"Come and show yourself, witch," he said quietly. "Everyone is asleep. If you wish to speak to me privately, now is the time."

Cooper glimpsed a hint of movement to his right as Shirell appeared at the edge of the trees. To anyone else, she would have been just another shadow caused by the flickering firelight.

"Guardian, I would offer you a trade," she said.

"What is it that you wish to trade for?" Cooper asked.

"I have knowledge that may be very useful to you. Information about the hooded figure in the cave."

Cooper nodded. "That could be very helpful if we meet him again. But I have no gold or valuables. What would you ask for in exchange?"

"Your help. My leg was injured in the confrontation in the caves. Every day the pain becomes worse. It is widely known that you have been trained as a healer. I need you to treat it."

Cooper motioned for her to approach. "I will agree to try. I can't promise anything until I know how serious your injury is. Please, come into the firelight and allow me examine it."

Shirell's face twisted into a grimace as she hobbled over to where Cooper sat. He helped her to sit, and she moved her robe aside to reveal a leg that was swollen to twice its normal size and beginning to turn black between the ankle and the knee.

Anger flared in Cooper's eyes. "Foolish girl. You should have told me about this in the cave. There is an ooze produced by a poisonous fungus that grows on the caves' crystals and will infect even the smallest of cuts. It is transparent and difficult to see, but if you travel the caves often, you should have known about it. If you had waited another day, your stubbornness would have cost you the leg. Within three days, the infection would have killed you. If you believe in any gods, you should pray to them that I can stop this infection before it spreads any further."

Shirell felt like a scolded child. The shadow mage had warned her about the fungus, and she had carelessly forgotten. "I'm sorry. There was only a small cut, barely a scratch. I believed that otherwise it was just a bad bruise. I'm not used to asking for help. Can you heal it?"

"I think so, but I'll need a helper. I wish Mina was here. She is well trained and experienced. Fortunately for you, my daughter Elana has had some training. I will need you to wait here while I wake her. One other thing. I know that you feel you have a score to settle with the princess. As long as you are here, you will not attempt to harm her in any way. After we have gone our separate ways, you may do as you wish, but if you truly want my help, you will restrain yourself. Otherwise, I will stand aside and let the infection run its course. By morning, you won't be able to stand, and soon after that, you'll die screaming in pain. Agreed?"

"I seem to have little choice," Shirell said with a shrug. "I will do nothing to harm the princess. You have my word. Just don't ask me to curtsy when she comes by." Cooper rose, went to where Elana was sleeping, and silently woke her. In a whisper, he explained the situation. She was up in an instant. She gasped when she saw Shirell's leg but said nothing as she quickly laid out a blanket and helped Shirell into a seated position. She quietly told Shirell that she would sit behind her to support her and help her to remain still.

Just as Cooper was ready to begin, Shirell spoke up. "I would offer you a second trade. The secret to traversing the Ice Caves safely if you will show me what you do. Teach me."

Surprise was evident on the faces of both Cooper and Elana.

"Well...I didn't expect that. Healing skills are a valuable thing. If you truly wish to learn, I will show you. The process is not complicated, but it does require precise control of the magic. If your skills are not adequate, you will do more harm than good," replied Cooper.

"I am well practiced at controlling my magic, Guardian," Shirell answered. "And I will follow your instructions precisely. It is my leg that you're working on, and I have no wish to be crippled."

"Very well then. If you have your talisman, we can begin," Cooper said as he jammed his staff into the soft ground next to Shirell. The staff stood upright and shone a soft blue light that illuminated the small area surrounding them. Shirell brought out her talisman, which was already glowing. With a skeptical eye, Cooper looked at the makeshift amberstone formed from shards of stone lashed together, but he said nothing.

"First, we must be able to see the problem." Cooper

then slowly spoke three words that were like nothing Shirell had ever heard before. "These words are in the ancient language of the high elves. They will do no harm. Depending on how they are said, they can make an object invisible for a short time. You must say them just loud enough and slowly enough to make only the skin vanish so that we may see what is beneath."

As Cooper spoke, Shirell's leg began to shimmer and the skin seemed to fade as the sinews and tendons began to reveal themselves. Shirell shuddered as she saw what was beneath the skin. The muscles were spider-webbed with black lines where the infection had spread.

"See how the poison follows the blood vessels as it spreads? Soon, it would have invaded the main artery going to your heart. Then there would have been no stopping it. What we must do is go to the very end of each trail of infection. Pinpoint your magic on the blackened end of every blood vessel and slowly push the poison back to its source. It will not be easy. You must push upstream, against the natural direction that the blood would flow."

"I understand," Shirell answered. "Let me try."

A pencil thin beam of blue light shone from her finger as Shirell slowly traced the line of a blood vessel. Tiny beads of sweat formed on her forehead as the black line gradually turned pink and the infection receded from the magic.

"Good," Cooper said. "Keep your light steady. If you stray from the infection, you may damage the tissue beneath. Do another one while I observe, and then I will begin from the opposite end and we will both work toward the center."

Shirell nodded her understanding, and for the next twenty minutes they worked silently, steadily pushing the infection back to the spot where it began. Elana regularly wiped Shirell's face with a damp cloth as the exertion began to show, but Shirell kept her hand steady until finally only a tiny black spot remained.

"Excellent," Cooper said. "We're almost finished. This is the worst part. I need to burn off the infection and seal the cut. I'm sorry, but this will hurt, and I need you to remain perfectly still. I will be as quick as possible. Elana will help steady you. Are you ready?"

Shirell's voice was raspy, but determination showed on her face as she said, "I'm ready, finish it."

Shirell's mouth opened in a silent scream and she squeezed Elana's hand hard enough to make her eyes water, but Shirell didn't flinch as Cooper focused the blue light of his magic on the small black line of infection and began to burn it off. Within ten seconds, a tiny wisp of smoke curled upward and Cooper announced, "There, it's done. You will have a small scar and you will need to rest for a day before walking, but otherwise your leg should recover fully. There is a small protected grove of trees a hundred yards to the west where you can rest safely, and I will have Quisp come and protect you. He will guard you with his life."

Shirell offered no objections but watched intently as Elana swabbed and dressed the small wound with skilled hands.

"It's a clean wound, it should heal quickly," said Elana.

"You seem to have some experience at this. Thank you for your help."

"Years ago, I spent some time working as a nurse to help pay for my education," Elana answered. "Now, if you really want to thank me, listen to my father and get some sleep."

Cooper picked her up and gently carried her to the hidden spot he had found. Elana followed with a blanket, then quickly went to fetch Quisp.

By the time Quisp arrived, Shirell was nearly asleep from exhaustion. Cooper promised to come and speak to her in the morning, and she whispered a feeble, "Thank you." Just before she allowed herself to sleep, she looked up at Quisp and said, "Don't you dare call me mistress!"

The shadow mage smiled wickedly under his hood as he peered through the trees. He couldn't have planned it better. There was the little witch, Shirell, asleep under a tree. She had not been hard to find. He had been able to sense the traces of magic from miles away. The bandage on her leg confirmed his suspicion that she had been injured in the cave. And she was being guarded by an old elf. He had changed his name and appearance over the years, but the mage still recognized him. Quisp was the name that he had used during the war, and he had been a constant source of interference. There were still some gremlin sympathizers who would pay handsomely for his demise. A choking mist would easily be mistaken for a bit of early morning fog until it was too late.

Faint wisps of smoke began to curl away from the wizard's hands as he whispered the chant. They snaked across the glade, blending with the mist coming off the grass until they encircled the unsuspecting elf and coalesced around his mouth and nose. Quisp was unaware of the mist until he began to gasp, his lungs starving for air, but by then, he was unable to cry out. He tried to rise, but the lack of air had sapped his strength. He sagged back against the tree trunk, desperately struggling for breath, but it was too late. His feet twitched once, and then he was still.

"So much for the elf," the mage whispered to himself as the ribbons of blue smoke slipped away from Quisp and started toward Shirell. "Now, witch, let me show you what happens to those who turn against me."

Ashley smiled as she watched the rabbit slowly inch out into the open. She had already gotten two of his companions, and a third would make a fine breakfast for the group. When Bodkin had come to relieve her at dawn, Ashley mentioned that roasted rabbit would be a nice change from the bread and dried fruit that they had gotten from a local farmer. The elf girl immediately agreed and offered to let the princess use her bow.

As Ashley walked, she examined the borrowed

weapon with a practiced eye. It was well crafted and had excellent balance. It felt natural in her hands. The princess hadn't gone on an early morning hunt for a long time, and it felt good. A chance to be alone and clear her head.

Was it wrong for her to hope that this little trip would last a bit longer? She had forgotten how much she enjoyed Cooper's company. His quiet strength and good humor always put her at ease and was certainly a pleasant change from dealing with court officials and her father's unpredictable moods. They had been in love once when they were young, and she had ruined that. Then he had fallen in love with Anna and she had been happy for both of them. But Anna was gone now, and Cooper was alone. Was there still a spark between them? Ashley had never married. She had male friends, some of whom would have married her in an instant, but none of them had ever seemed quite right.

Ashley had always had a strained relationship with her niece Elana. Even Ashley had to admit that they were too much alike. Both of them were a little too headstrong. They clashed every time they were together. But Ashley adored Susan. Watching Susan and Bodkin together reminded her of her days growing up with Anna.

Ashley knew that Cooper would never relinquish his duty as a guardian to come and be with her at Kestriana and, unlike her sister, Ashley couldn't go and live in the human world, but perhaps he would come and visit more often now that the king had had a change of heart after meeting his great-granddaughter.

When she finally looked up from her musings, the rabbit had wandered completely across the clearing to the far side, and she no longer had a clear shot. She cursed under her breath. Foolish young girl daydreams. Now, she would have to hope that the rabbit stayed there while she circled around and tried to get a shot from the opposite side.

Quiet as a ghost, she eased around a large juniper

bush, trying to get a better angle. A snicker in the tree to her left chattered noisily. As she turned to shoo the little pest away, she glanced into the glade and couldn't believe the scene before her.

Quisp was seated, his back against a tree. His face was blue and he wasn't moving. Not far from him was the witch that they had encountered in the cave lying on a blanket, her face slowly being covered with a blue fog of magic. She looked like she was beginning to choke. Opposite Quisp, the dark wizard that had attacked them in the Ice Caves was stalking slowly toward the helpless witch.

He may have already killed Quisp, there was no way for her to tell, but now he was using magic to strangle the girl! Witch or not, the young woman had tried to help them in the caves, and Ashley was not going to stand by and allow her to be murdered right in front of her.

The wizard was off at an angle and hadn't seen Ashley. It was a tricky shot, but the girl would die if Ashley hesitated. The twang of the bowstring was just loud enough for the mage to hear. He ducked at the last instant and the arrow passed through the top of his cowl, pining it to the tree behind him and tangling him in his hood off as he dodged out of the way. For just a second, his face was revealed. Instantly he reached up, tore his hood free from the tree, and fled into the brush.

Ashley shouted a warning cry used by the wardens of the forest to alert Bodkin as she raced to the witch's side. There was no time to chase after the wizard. The girl was still unable to breathe. The mage was gone, but the choking mist remained around the witch's face. Ashley had left everything back at the camp. She had no talisman with her and no time to wait for Cooper to come and help. Even if she found the witch's talisman, it would be tuned to the individual and she couldn't use it. Every talisman slowly became accustomed to its user. Others could use it, but it would take time for it to adjust to someone new. Time that she didn't have. Her only chance was to somehow wake the witch and hope that she would still be strong enough to the break the spell. Ashley grabbed her by the shoulders and shook her, but to no avail. In desperation, she found the girl's talisman hanging on a cord around her neck, placed it in the witch's hand, and slapped her hard across the face. The backlash from the magic threw Ashley backwards, and she found herself seated on the grass six feet away feeling like she had been kicked by a horse. But she could hear the witch coughing and gasping. She was awake and breathing!

Cooper burst through the trees, his staff glowing bright blue, as Ashley got to her feet.

"Check on Quisp," she said, pointing to where the old elf lay slumped against the tree. "He doesn't look good."

Cooper knelt next to Quisp for a moment before looking over at Ashley and shaking his head.

"I'm sorry. There's nothing I can do for him," he said.

Ashley quickly relayed all that had happened to Cooper. Her method was unconventional, but Ashley's quick thinking had saved the witch's life.

He glanced over at Shirell, who had nearly recovered. "It's a long story. Her name is Shirell. Let me tell her about Quisp. She won't like it, and I don't know what she'll do. I think she was beginning to trust me, but Quisp was one of her only true friends."

"Cooper, there was one other thing...I saw his face!"

"You saw the wizard's face?" Cooper asked. "Did you recognize him?"

"Yes, but you're not going to believe me when I tell you. I still can't believe it, and I saw him. It was my uncle."

Cooper stared at her in total disbelief. "Marcus, the king's brother? But that's not possible."

"I know that, but I swear that it was him."

"All right, go back to the camp and let them know

what's happened. Don't mention that you saw his face. I'll talk to Shirell and be there soon."

Cooper heard Shirell gasp and spun round to find her kneeling next to Quisp. She gently passed her hand over his face, closing his eyes before she slowly stood. The blackness in her eyes looked like it could burn a hole right through him.

"He did this, didn't he?" she asked, in a voice that was barely a hiss.

"Yes, the wizard from the caves paid you a visit. Who is he, and why does he want you dead?"

"He calls himself a shadow mage," Shirell said. "Beyond that, I don't know who he is. I've never seen his face. He used to be my teacher."

"A shadow mage?" Cooper asked in disbelief. "Are you sure?"

"Yes, I'm sure," Shirell answered. "Does that name mean something?"

"It used to," Cooper responded, shaking his head. "The Cult of the Shadow Mages was wiped out twenty years before the Gremlin War. They were originally an offshoot of the Guild of Conjurers, then they slowly began delving into darker and more dangerous magic. The guild ordered them to disband, but some of them continued to meet and experiment with dark forces in secret. Eventually, in their lust for power, they went too far and foolishly called up a demon that they couldn't control. The creature turned on them, draining their life force and devouring the entire group. The all died in screaming terror. It required the combined efforts of the orcanus and more than half the members of the guild to finally return the monster to the nether-world where it came from. If he's adopted the title shadow mage and is trying to revive the cult, he is a fool and a madman and he must be stopped."

"Agreed. I'm joining your group. When we find him, he'll pay for what he's done to Quisp," Shirell said, then quietly added, "Thank you for saving my life."

"I didn't. The princess saved you," Cooper answered. "She gambled that slapping you would shock your reflexes into using the magic to protect yourself and break free of the mist. She took quite a chance, risking that you might also kill her in the process. You're both lucky that she guessed correctly."

Shirell was silent as they went to find the others.

The travelers remained in the glen with Quisp for the rest of the day. They had no tools to bury him, so much of the morning was spent collecting stones that were used to cover and protect the body from animals. After initial introductions, Shirell stationed herself next to Quisp. She offered to help collect stones, but Cooper insisted that if she wished to travel with them, she needed to stay off the injured leg, so he put her in charge of the placement of the stones. She spoke very little, usually directing the others with her hands or a nod.

After a simple lunch, Elana took the two girls for a walk while Cooper and the princess went to speak with Shirell. Her eyes were guarded as the princess sat on a stump facing her. The witch had given her word that she would not attempt to harm Ashley, but Cooper was still unsure how she would react to being this close to her.

"Thank you, Princess, for your help," Shirell said quietly with a glance at Cooper. "I would be there next to Quisp if not for your quick thinking."

"I couldn't stand by and let him kill you right in front of me," Ashley responded. "And you did help us in the caves. It seems that we have a common enemy. Let me tell you what we know, then anything that you can tell us will help us plan what to do next. Cooper said that you only know this wizard as the shadow mage. I was able to get a look at his face when he was attacking you. His name is Marcus Samarian. He is the king's brother and my uncle."

"Are you certain of this?"

"I can barely believe it myself, but yes, I saw him quite clearly, and I've seen his face thousands of times growing up in the castle. It was my uncle."

"I was unaware that the king had a brother," Shirell said.

"That is not surprising. He is not spoken of much. My Uncle Marcus was wild and troublesome as a young man, never listening to anyone. When he was nineteen, he ignored the stable master's warnings and decided that since he was a prince of the royal family, then he should be entitled to ride the biggest stallion in the stable. The horse was far too much for him to handle, and it threw him. He landed hard and his head struck a rock. For two days, the healers didn't know if he would live or die. He survived, but he didn't speak for another two weeks. When he did finally speak, they discovered that the blow to his head had robbed him of his senses and he now had the mind of a child. He spent most of his time wandering aimlessly around the castle, sometimes picking wild flowers and dropping them in the nearby stream to watch them float away. Five years ago, the servant who usually watched him was suddenly taken ill. The guards in the castle were new and unaware of Marcus's habit of slipping out of his room and walking the castle halls late at night. With no one to stop him, he wandered out of the castle and off into the forest. They found what they thought was him two days later. A pack of nightshade dogs had discovered him alone in the woods and torn him to pieces. His body was terribly mangled and his face unrecognizable. . We had to identify him by his tattered clothing. He always wore a deep blue tunic, the trademark color of the royal family. His signet ring was still on what remained of his hand. Although no one blamed him, the poor servant was so devastated that he had failed in his duty that he later took his own life."

"You believe that he recovered from his injury and has just been pretending to be a fool for many years?" Shirell asked "A clever disguise. No one pays much attention to what they say near a fool. And you believe that he also faked his own death?"

"I'm certain of it now." Ashley said. "He carries the Dragon Staff. It disappeared many years ago from a vault deep under the castle. The vault is only opened once a year to inventory the contents, so no one knows exactly when it was stolen. But it had to have been taken by someone in the castle. No outsider would be able to find the vault. I can count on one hand the number of people who know the vault's location. It is possible that my uncle may have followed one of them to the secret hiding place. He was often found wandering the lower halls of the castle, and no one paid any attention to him. The Dragon Staff was a symbol of authority carried by the orcanus, the leader of the Guild of Conjurors, and passed down from one leader to the next. It can strengthen magic and increase its power. Very few people even knew of the staff's existence. After the war, all but a very select few were told that it was destroyed in the devastation of the hall."

"I remember the first time he showed it to me," Shirell answered with a nod. "He was elated that he had gotten it. All that you have said makes sense. When I was his student years ago, it was common not to see him for days at a time. That must have been times when the servant was watching him closely. Something in his past has caused him to hate his brother, the king. He would sometimes go on endlessly about destroying the king and bringing the entire kingdom to its knees. To that end, he searches for other magic artifacts, especially something called the Eye of Bangor Khan. He believes that once he has that, nothing can stand in his way."

Cooper whistled quietly "He could be right. Where the Dragon Staff amplifies magic, the eye neutralizes it. If he was to activate it near the Barrier, all the evil creatures trapped in the Land of Non could be released. This entire world would be devastated, and if some of the creatures managed to escape into the human world, it could also be destroyed. But the eye has been lost for decades."

"Isn't that what they said about the Dragon Staff?"

Shirell asked.

"Yes, you're right. But the eye vanished long before the war. Anyone who even might have known anything about it is long dead, and its hiding place would have been protected with the strongest of spells to keep it from being located. No one would even know where to begin to search for it. It will never be found."

"I hope you're right, Guardian."

Chapter 8

In the morning, the travelers started off again in search of Horus's cabin. Cooper took the lead with Shirell, the newest addition to their group, covering the rear and constantly on the watch for an ambush. If the injured leg bothered her, she was not letting anyone know. Her anger at Quisp's murder had become fierce determination. She was going to find the shadow mage and make him pay for what he had done.

By late morning, they began to hear a rumbling off in the distance.

Susan moved up to walk next to Cooper.

"Grandfather, is someone coming? It sounds like horses."

"No, Susan, That sound just means that we're getting close to the river. That's why they call it the Equus. Equus is a word for horses. Certain sections of the river contain a lot of rocks and small rapids, so as you approach, it sounds like horses galloping towards you. I hope we can find a shallow place to cross without having to go too far downstream. We should be able to see the river very soon."

Cooper's assessment was correct. A few moments later, the forest opened onto a sandy riverbank. Just as Cooper had stated, the river was littered with boulders and rapids of all different sizes and shapes swirled amid the rocks. Traveling this part of the river by boat or raft would be impossible.

"It's been a long time, but I believe I recognize this

spot," Cooper said. "If we follow the riverbank for about a quarter mile, there should be a shallow spot where we may be able to cross. Horus's cabin should only be about two miles downstream from there."

Elana slipped up alongside of Cooper and whispered in his ear, "Dad, she's trying to hide it, but Shirell is starting to noticeably limp on that sore leg. Why don't we take a ten minute break here?"

"Sounds like a good idea. I was going to suggest that I go up to the next bend in the river and scout ahead. Why don't you tell the others? Shirell seems friendly towards Susan. Why don't you take her with you to look at the dressing on that leg? Shirell may have developed an infection. It could be a good opportunity to show Susan what to look for and maybe build a little trust with the witch."

When Cooper returned after ten minutes, Elana walked down to meet him.

"How does our young witch's leg wound look?" he asked.

"It seems to be healing nicely. I think you were right. Shirell does seem to like Susan. She let her change the dressing without any objection. How does it look downstream?"

"Good and bad. The good news is that a hundred yards past the bend, the riverbed clears and there are very few rocks beyond that point. The bad thing is that the water gets much deeper, and with no rocks to slow it down, the current immediately begins to pick up speed. There is a very small shallow spot where I believe I can get across with a rope. Although it would be difficult, the adults could probably wade across, but it's too deep and the current is much too strong for the girls. Once we have a rope strung across, I think we should be able to get them across safely."

"All right, let's rest another five minutes, then I'll tell the others and we'll get started again."

It only took fifteen minutes to hike downstream to

the spot that Cooper had described. Once the river made the bend, the riverbed turned to sand and quickly dropped to about eight feet deep as the water became a raging torrent. The transition between the two sections of the river was a shallow section only about ten feet wide.

Cooper tied the rope around his waist, removed his boots and, jamming his staff into the riverbed to help steady himself against the current, he started across.

Both Ashley and Elana held the end of the rope and slowly played it out as Cooper started across. They were taking no chances that he might get swept away if he lost his footing. It was clearly a struggle crossing against the fast moving current, and it took Cooper ten minutes to fight his way across. By the time he made it to the opposite shore, he had been pushed downstream until he was at the very edge of the drop-off, but he made it.

The women tied the end of the rope to a nearby tree until most of them could cross. The last one over would tie it around her waist to cross. The rope was a valuable item. They didn't want to abandon it.

"There's nothing close by to anchor the rope to. I'll just have to hold it," Cooper called from across the water as he planted his feet in the sand and took up the slack.

They decided that the safest way to cross was to keep the girls between the adults. Ashley went first, followed by Bodkin, then Elana, then Susan, and Shirell last.

Ashley and Bodkin made it across without incident. Elana was two feet from shore and Susan and Shirell were just starting across when Elana looked up and let out a quiet gasp at what she saw. Out of nowhere, twin fawns had suddenly appeared ten feet from Cooper's right. They had all been so preoccupied with crossing the river that no one had seen the deer come out of the trees. They wobbled on pencil thin legs as they bent to drink from the water.

"They're beautiful," Ashley whispered a split second before a bolt of brown fur shot out of the trees and headbutted Cooper squarely in the chest. He flew three feet, landing face first in the water. The angry doe pawed at the ground and refused to let him back on shore.

"She must think that we're threatening the young ones!" Elana cried.

"The rope!" Cooper sputtered as he tried to spit out a mouthful of river water.

Ashley lunged for the end of the rope, but the big doe was in front of her and snorted menacingly. While they watched helplessly, the end of the rope snaked into the water and the current carried it away.

As the rope suddenly went slack, both Susan and Shirell were thrown off balance, and the fast moving current instantly swept them off their feet and began to carry them downstream. Shirell struggled to keep her head above water while frantically hauling in on the rope to draw Susan to her. She silently thanked her mother for forcing her to learn to swim when she was a girl. She hadn't wanted to bother at the time, but Kiri had insisted.

After what seemed like an eternity, Shirell caught Susan's arm and dragged her in close. They both realized that their chances were better together than separate. Now if they could just keep their heads above water in this breakneck current long enough to get to shore.

The two clung desperately to each other as the fast moving water bounced and buffeted them. It was impossible to swim against the current. The best they could manage was to just keep from getting pulled under.

"Susan!" Elana frantically screamed as she watched the two being carried around the bend and out of sight.

Cooper was finally able to drag himself from the shallows as the angry doe herded her two young ones back into the trees, but by then, it was too late. Susan and Shirell were gone.

Elana grabbed Cooper by the arm. "Dad, we have to go after them!"

"We will," he answered, shaking off the water from the river. "Is everyone else all right?"

Ashley and Bodkin nodded. They had already gathered all their gear and were ready to immediately start after Susan and Shirell.

"I've followed this section of the river before. It moves very fast for the next mile or two before it begins to widen and slow down. Fortunately, there's no rocks. I don't know about the witch, but Susan's a good swimmer. As long as they can keep their heads above water, they should be able to ride the current and get to shore once the river slows. We'll follow the river and we should find them. There's going to be places where the forest comes right down to the shoreline and there's no riverbank. We'll have to detour through the woods. It'll slow us down a bit, but as long as we keep moving, we should be able to catch up to them quickly. With a little luck, they'll wash up near Horus's cabin. C'mon, my clothes will dry as we walk."

Ashley had retrieved Cooper's staff when the deer attacked. She handed it back to him as they started off downstream.

Shirell and Susan were bruised and battered by the time the river slowed. At a bend, they were deposited on a shallow sand bar where they could finally drag themselves to shore. Both were exhausted from the ordeal, and neither one said a word as they sat on the sand, catching their breath.

Finally, Shirell spoke up. "Susan, are you hurt at all?"

"No, I don't think so, just cold and wet. That water was freezing."

"Yes, it was. We need to collect some driftwood and start a fire to dry our clothes, but we have nothing dry to change into."

"I have some clothes in my backpack that are in waterproof bags. I'm sure that none of my stuff will fit you, but I have a blanket that you could cover yourself with."

"As long as it's dry, a blanket would be fine. Thank

you. Years ago, I was forced to survive in the woods and my clothes were so ragged and torn that I was almost naked most of the time. How in the world were you able to keep from losing that pack in the water?"

"I don't know for sure. My arms were through the straps, and we never let go of each other long enough for it to slip off. I think you saved my life."

"We saved each other. The bags in your pack must have some air in them. Your pack was helping us stay afloat. And the blanket will keep me from freezing to death. If your grandfather follows the river, they should find us, but there's no way to tell how far we were carried by that current or how long that may take." Shirell looked around at the empty riverbank. "That old wizard's cabin was supposed to be near here, but we may have been swept right on past it. We should build a fire, dry our clothes, and rest a bit while we wait. If they don't find us by the time our clothes are dry, we can start back upstream along the riverbank. We can't really get lost, and we should meet up with them as long as they stick to the river."

"That all sounds good," Susan said as she dumped the contents of her backpack on the sandy riverbank. Mina had helped her seal most of her gear in re-sealable plastic bags in case they got caught in the rain and, amazingly, it was still dry. She had a change of clothes, the blanket that she had promised to Shirell, a bag of trail mix that Mina had prepared for her, and her boomerang.

"What's the funny looking stick for?" Shirell asked.

"It's a boomerang, a throwing stick. It's curved that way so that when you throw it, it arcs around and comes back. I brought it along because Bodkin and I like to throw it. It's just for fun."

Shirell looked over the boomerang with a skeptical eye. "A stick that comes back when you throw it? Without using magic? Sounds strange. You'll have to show me how that works while we're waiting. C'mon, let's collect some wood and get a fire started."

The sandbar was littered with driftwood that the river had thrown up at the bend. Within minutes, they had enough for a fire. As Shirell lit the fire with a few sparks of magic, Susan got a look at her talisman.

"That's the most unusual amberstone I've ever seen. Where did you get it?"

Shirell hesitated before answering. She didn't like talking about her past, but it was an innocent question, and something about Susan told her that there was no reason not to trust her. Maybe it was the fact that she and Susan had almost drown together. She just didn't know, but, after a moment's pause, she answered Susan's question openly.

"When I was just a little older than you, I went to study at the Hall of Conjurors. I know that your grandfather's told about the Gremlin War years ago. Well, I was trapped inside the wreckage of the hall for three days after it was attacked and destroyed by the monster known as the lindworm. I eventually managed to escape, but by then, I was nearly starving and the Gremlin Army was still close by. So I hid in the woods near the hall and scavenged whatever I could. As I dug through the rubble looking for food, I kept finding small shards from shattered amberstones. I collected as many pieces as I could and eventually bound them all together. It works as a talisman, but sometimes the magic is unstable. I have to be very careful. If I try too hard, the stone kicks some of the magic back at me. It's burned my hand a few times." Shirell paused for a moment. "That fire seems to be going good, and I've talked about myself for too long. I'm sorry, Susan, I don't like talking about those days, and I'm freezing in these wet clothes. If you give me that blanket, I'll take them off and we can stretch them out in front of this fire and let them dry."

Susan had been so intent on Shirell's story that she had forgotten that they were both still soaking wet. She immediately jumped up and grabbed the blanket.

"You go first," Shirell said "There's some bushes

over there that you can change behind. You have dry clothes, and I'll need the blanket to cover up with. I'll stand watch while you change."

Susan nodded and slipped behind the bushes to change. Once she was out of sight, she immediately checked the small pouch that the Spirit of the Golden Willow had given to her. The amberstone was still safely tucked inside. She had tried to keep a hand on it while they were in the river, but they had been tumbled around so much that she was afraid that the magic stone may have fallen out. Once she was sure that it was safe, she quickly changed and returned to where Shirell waited.

With the blanket in hand, it was Shirell's turn behind the bushes. She quickly returned with her wet clothes along with a few long thin branches and some small vines that she turned into a tripod.

Now that Shirell was barefoot and wrapped only in a blanket, Susan noticed that Shirell was much smaller and more petite than she normally appeared with her imposing robe and boots. Shirell had inherited her mother's raven black hair and dark eyes, but with her hair wet and pulled back, Susan could see the traces of elf blood in the slightly pointed ears and the delicate features. Shirell had also inherited the elven trait of slow aging. Even though she had been a girl during the Gremlin Wars forty years ago, she only appeared to be a young woman in her twenties.

With their clothes spread out on the tripod to dry, Susan and Shirell sat on a large rock near the fire warming themselves and sharing the bag of trail mix from Susan's pack. They sat quietly for a short time as neither one was sure what to say to the other. Susan quickly became bored with the silence, so when a small, raccoon-like animal came to drink from the river on the opposite shore, she asked if Shirell knew what it was called. Without realizing it, Susan had stumbled on the right subject. Shirell had always had a gift for communicating with animals, and she began to talk about Pinkie, her little snicker friend.

"Pinkie was somewhere nearby in the trees when we got to the river," Shirell said. "Sooner or later, he'll find me. He always does."

Susan began to tell Shirell about Cookie, her grandfather's dog, and for nearly an hour they traded stories and chatted like old friends, almost forgetting that they had nearly drowned in the river. Then Shirell remembered the boomerang.

"Hey, weren't you going to show me how that funny looking throwing stick works?"

"You're right, I almost forgot. C'mon, we need to go where there's an open area on the riverbank."

Twenty yards downstream, the bank opened up to about fifty yards wide. Susan spent the next half hour showing Shirell how to throw the boomerang and have it circle back. Shirell's attempts to throw it were less than stellar. Her last throw wobbled erratically and barely missed hitting her in the ankle when it came back.

"You're clearly much better at this than I am," Shirell admitted. "I'll stick to magic. We should check on our clothes. They should be dry by now, and we can start back to try to meet up with your grandfather and the rest."

Shirell was right; their clothes were dry. They quickly changed, put out the fire, packed the few things that they had, and started the hike back upstream.

Cooper and company had gone about three quarters of a mile along the riverbank before the trees came right down to the water and they were forced to detour into the woods. Their only choice was a faint trail leading away from the river.

"As long as we can hear the river, we should still be able to follow it. Watch for side trails. I believe that this may be one of Horus's trails. I'm sure that we're close to his cabin."

Cooper was right. A few hundred yards up the trail, Bodkin found an offshoot trail.

"This should be the path that leads to Horus's cabin. I'm certain of it," Cooper said.

"But, Dad, we have to find Susan," Elana reminded him.

"I know, but it's also imperative that we find Horus, especially if Marcus has the Dragon Staff and is also looking for him. We'll only take five minutes to go down this trail. If we find Horus, Ashley can stay and explain everything that's happened. Hopefully, he'll be cooperative and she won't have too much trouble convincing him to help us. He may even have some idea of where to look for Susan and Shirell. Whether we find him or not, I'll double back and continue searching. Susan is smart, and I have a feeling that Shirell is pretty resourceful. If they're hurt, they'll stay put and wait for us; otherwise, they'll stay close to the river and follow it back upstream. We'll find them." As predicted, a few hundred yards up the trail they found Horus's cottage. The trail opened up into a clearing, and the small cabin sat at the opposite end.

"I don't like this," Cooper said as they started across the glen. "There's no protections or safeguards around the cabin. Horus would never leave his home completely unprotected like this. Everyone keep your wits about you. This smells like —"

Ashley finished his sentence for him as she yelled, "It's a trap, get down!" and tackled him from behind. On the way to the ground, he could feel the heat as the ball of blue fire singed the hair on top of his head.

The shadow mage appeared off to the left of the cottage, his hood up, concealing his face. He brandished the Dragon Staff as he prepared another strike.

Bodkin was instantly on one knee firing a steady stream of arrows at him as quickly as she could. Her missiles were harmlessly deflected by the magic emanating from the Dragon Staff, but it distracted the wizard long enough for Cooper and Ashley to get to their feet and race to the relative safety of the trees.

The wizard continued the onslaught for the next few

minutes, relentlessly hurling blue fire at the travelers as they scrambled to protect themselves.

When he finally stopped, Cooper called out to him, "There's no need for the hood, Marcus. Your secret is out. We know who you are."

With his free hand, the wizard yanked back his hood to reveal a face twisted into a sneer. "And I know who you are, Cooper, the exalted human hero of the Gremlin Wars. Cooper the warrior who disgraced himself by running off with the king's daughter. Exiled from the kingdom of the elves and reduced to being a lowly gatekeeper. And now you return for the other princess? Is there no end to your arrogance? Give me the Eye of Bangor Khan, Gatekeeper, and I'll spare your world. I'll even allow you to take my niece along with you when you return home."

"The blow to your head still clouds your thinking, Marcus. You call yourself a shadow mage. Do you know nothing of the shadow mages of old? Their lust for power destroyed them all. The eye was lost decades ago, and I wouldn't give it to you even if I did have it. Using it to release the demons trapped behind the Barrier would be madness. Even with the Dragon Staff, you couldn't control them. No one could."

"You lie!" Marcus screamed. "The necromancer, Eldred, used the Dragon Staff and the amberstone to capture and control the creatures when he created the Barrier. And you, my friend, were his favorite student. If he was to tell anyone of the location of the eye's hiding place, it would be you."

"You're wrong, Marcus. He never told me."

"Once again, you tell lies," Marcus hissed. "Give me the location of the eye and go free. Refuse and I will eliminate your family and friends, including your newest love interest, Princess Ashley, right before your eyes. Then I will kill you, find the eye, and destroy my brother. He'll pay for his crimes."

"The king spent years making sure that you were

well cared for. What crimes has he committed, Marcus?"

"Fool!" Marcus shrieked. "Don't pretend ignorance with me! He stole my kingdom. It was my birthright."

"No, Marcus, it was not. Marinus was the elder brother. He was the proper heir to the throne. If you destroy the Barrier, the creatures behind it will devastate the kingdom. Even if you succeed in destroying the king, there will be nothing left to rule. Your plan cannot work."

"Liar! I will regain what is mine. But you will not survive to see it!" Marcus shouted as he renewed his assault on Cooper and the rest.

The riverbank steadily tapered down until it was barely wide enough for Susan and Shirell to walk single file before finally ending in a briar patch at the water's edge.

"I guess we have no choice but to follow the trail," Shirell said, pointing to a narrow opening between two oaks.

Susan shrugged. She didn't want to get too far from the river, but there was no other option.

"If the trail leads too far into the woods and away from the river, we'll turn back," Shirell added.

They had been walking for a half an hour listening for the river when the trail split. One leg seemed to head back toward the river, and the other deeper into the woods. But they could hear sounds in the direction of the second trail.

"That might be my grandfather."

"Maybe it's them and they've found Horus's cabin. But maybe not. We should approach carefully. We're on the edge of gnome territory, and some of them aren't very friendly towards humans or elves."

Susan did remember her grandfather saying that, so they went silently up the trail, watching for any movement and following the sounds ahead.

When they saw the opening in the woods ahead, they slipped off the trail and cautiously approached through the trees until they could see the clearing. From where they watched, they could see Cooper, Princess Ashley, and Elana all trying desperately to ward off the bolts of blue magic lightning being thrown at them by the shadow mage. Any counterattack they attempted bounced harmlessly off a protective shield emanating from the Dragon Staff.

"We have to help them!" Susan desperately whispered.

"We will, but we can't just attack him. We won't do any better than the others if we do that. We need a plan. I have an idea. Quisp told me that you are the niece of the princess. Is that true?" Shirell asked.

"Yes, my grandmother was Princess Ashley's sister."

"Then you are of royal blood. Can you do red magic?"

"Yes, I've done a little, but I don't think it will help us. I can't use it to hurt people. I haven't been through the kuri-aken ritual."

"That doesn't matter," Shirell said. "All we need is a distraction. Look at the strain on his face. He's holding off three people. Even with the Dragon Staff, that requires a lot of concentration. If you infuse your throwing stick with red magic, it will be able to pass through his shield of magic. It doesn't have to hurt him, just distract him. If he loses his focus, one of us will be able to break through his shield and stop him."

Susan grabbed her boomerang with one hand and retrieved the small round amberstone that the Spirit of the Golden Willow had given her from the pouch around her neck.

A sly smile crossed Shirell face as she recognized the stone. "The ancient tree spirit gave you that stone, didn't she? I was watching from a distance that night, but the spirit kept you shrouded in mist. And you've kept it a secret up till now. You're a smart girl, Susan, but you need to use that stone now."

Shirell was right. This was why the Spirit of the Golden Willow had given her the stone. Her family, friends, and this entire world were in danger. She knew what she had to do.

The boomerang in her hand instantly began to glow red. As Susan concentrated on it, the wood seemed to absorb the light like a sponge. Once the boomerang had returned to its normal appearance, she stepped out into the open.

"No, Susan!" Cooper shouted from across the glade. Both he and the women stopped their assault when they saw Susan at the edge of the clearing.

A wicked smile crossed the face of the shadow mage as he saw Susan.

"Now you send a mere child out to face me? Oh, Cooper, you must be desperate indeed."

"Leave her alone, Marcus," Cooper snarled at him. "Susan, get back, he's too dangerous."

Susan didn't like ignoring her grandfather, but she stood her ground. "Hello, I'm Susan, the king's great-granddaughter. That must make you my Uncle Marcus."

"Who you are is of no importance to me," Marcus sneered "If you're smart, you will run home to your human world, child. This world will soon belong to me, and I will rid it of my brother and his whole wretched family. Run, child, or be destroyed with them."

"No, I won't do that. And please stop calling me a child. I don't like that."

"And what do you propose to do about it, child?" the mage asked, laughing.

"I will stop you."

"Really? How will you do that, child? Throw your funny shaped stick at me? Your little elf friend tried her arrows, but they couldn't reach me."

"Maybe I'll have better luck," Susan said as she hurled the boomerang in the direction of the dark wizard.

It passed by him three feet to his right, and then began to arc around behind him.

"Is that the best you can do, child?" he taunted. "You need more practice. That wasn't even close."

"I'm sorry, I'll try to aim better next time," Susan answered as anger showed on her young face. "Oh, and Uncle Marcus...*don't call me a child!*"

As Susan defiantly faced down the wizard, the boomerang reached the top of its arc, reversed direction, and spun back toward the shadow mage. There was a tiny flicker of red light as the boomerang passed effortlessly through the protective shield of magic and slammed hard onto the mage's wrist. His magic faltered as the sudden shock and pain distracted the wizard and caused him to weaken his grip on the staff. From across the glade, Cooper had been watching the path of the boomerang and timed his strike to hit at just that instant. Cooper's blast shattered the wall of magic, and the Dragon Staff went skating across the grass as it was forcibly driven from the mage's hand.

The dark wizard stumbled back a step, stunned from the impact. Shirell stepped out into the open. Her hands crackled with blue fire as she summoned every ounce of magic she possessed into one huge fireball. "This is for Quisp, Master," she said, her words dripping with contempt for her former teacher. She hurled the ball of blue fire at him. It shot across the glade like a lightning bolt and exploded into a thousand blinding fireworks as it hit the mage square in the chest with the force of a battering ram. Shirell cried out in pain and grabbed her hand as her makeshift amberstone instantly shattered into dust from the intense backlash of her strike. The dark wizard was lifted off his feet and thrown ten feet into the air before slamming backwards into an enormous oak tree. He slid down the trunk of the tree, crumpled into a heap at its base, and didn't move as tiny wisps of smoke snaked upwards from the front of his robe.   After Marcus was bound and all his talismans removed to prevent him from using magic to try and escape, a message was sent to the castle. Shirell was able to charm a local raven and send him directly to Korin with a note, signed by the princess, attached to his leg. The bird returned in an hour with a reply saying that a full garrison was being dispatched to escort Marcus back to the castle.

Horus was found in his cottage, unharmed. Marcus had slipped past his defensive spells and come upon him while he slept. A simple spell that prevented him from waking was all Marcus had needed to subdue Horus.

After Horus was awakened and told of everything that had happened, it was difficult to tell what upset the old wizard more — the idea that he had been attacked in his own cottage, or the fact that dozens of strangers would now know where to find him.

A week after the capture of the shadow mage, a detail of six soldiers accompanied Shirell to the pauper's field where Kiri had been buried many years earlier. After the Gremlin Army had moved on, a group of local villagers had recovered her battered body from where the gremlins had abandoned her. They had carefully removed her body from the stake and wrapped it in oilcloth, the traditional method of preserving it, then buried her in a simple grave.

The soldiers carefully removed the body from the shallow grave. Then the old bones were gently transported to a secluded spot near the old farm where Kiri and her family had lived. A second group of soldiers was dispatched to retrieve Quisp's body and bring it to the same spot. All of Kiri's family were gone now, but Princess Ashley personally arranged for the farmer who now owned the property to sell them a small parcel of land, and he also agreed to maintain it.

Two days later, just after sunrise, Kiri and Quisp were quietly laid to rest, fulfilling a promise that Ashley had made to Shirell. A small group consisting of Cooper, Elana, Mina, Susan, and Bodkin all came. And from Kestriana, Princess Ashley came accompanied by Lady Coramina and Korin. The king even sent his personal emissary, Macilon, to pay his respects. Prax had temporarily returned from his search for more of his kind to honor the two. In a gesture of great respect usually reserved for kings and very special individuals, the great dragon circled overhead as Kiri and Quisp were being lowered into their new resting place, then landed off to the side, raised his head, and blew a plume of dragon fire hundreds of feet into the air. For miles in every direction, even as far away as the city of the elves, all who saw the flames knew that a person of honor had passed into the next life.

Shirell waited patiently until the elven burial detail finished their task, then she quietly thanked everyone, especially Susan, who seemed to have struck up a strong friendship with the witch during their time together.

"Where will you go now?" Susan asked.

"Home, at least for a short time. I have a small cabin hidden in the dark woods."

"Won't you be lonely all by yourself?"

"Well, I've been alone for a long time, but I will certainly miss Quisp and his wonderful chocolate. And Pinkie will be there to keep me company. I have a lot to think about. I promised Lady Coramina that I would come to the Castle of the Elves sometime soon and relate all that I know of the shadow mage to so she can enter it into the archives," Shirell answered. "And, after much persuasion, and the fact that we released him from the magic that imprisoned him in his cottage, Horus has consented to work with me to see if we can begin to rebuild the guild and preserve some of the old magic before it's lost forever. It will not be easy, neither of us is very good at dealing with people. We could use your grandfather's help. He is well respected and a good diplomat. We asked him, but he said that since Horus has restored the Gnome Door, he thought that it was time that he got back to his old job as guardian and the quiet of his workshop. He did offer to help as much as he can."

"Grandfather told me that we can come back and visit soon. I promise that I'll bring chocolate." Susan started to turn to go, then stopped. "Oh, could you keep this for us until we come back?" Susan placed an amberstone in Shirell's hand.

Shirell was almost speechless. "But the Spirit of the Golden Willow gave that to you. It should be yours to keep."

"Oh, I still have the small stone that the spirit gave me. This is the ancient amberstone that my grandfather has been keeping hidden for many years, hoping that someday the guild could be restored. Your stone was destroyed and the new orcanus, leader of the Guild of Conjurors, should have a proper stone, not a bunch of broken pieces. You have a lot of work to do. I think the spirit would approve."

For the first time since Susan had met her, a gentle smile crossed Shirell's face. "I don't know what to say except, thank you."

"My grandfather and my mom are anxious to go home. I have to go. I'll come back as soon as I can."

"I'll be waiting," Shirell said as she gave Susan's hand a gentle squeeze and sent her off to find Cooper, Elana, and Mina who were saying goodbye to Prax.

As Susan came over and hugged the dragon's huge neck, she said "Grandfather, I think I'm ready to go home now."

Tom Dillman started writing about a dozen years ago — he had stories in his head that he had to tell. In fact, The Gnome Door Chronicles began as a bedtime story and grew into a novel, and he is working on the next books in the series. He is retired and, when he's not writing, he enjoys woodworking. Dillman is also a long-time runner and student of karate. Dillman grew up in Reading, Pa., and is a 1974 graduate of Reading Senior High School. He has lived in Leesport, Pa., for over 25 years.

Printed in the USA
CPSIA information can be obtained
at www.ICGtesting.com
LVHW090000091224
798641LV00003B/590